V

at the X-Roads

He slowly unfolded the letter, took a deep breath and began to read. "What the hell?" He looked stupefied. He looked at me. "What is this?"

"I'm leaving you, Roger. It's over. I'm divorcing you." Oh, the sheer pleasure of finally pronouncing those words!

"But why?" he shrieked. "Why?"

"There are many reasons, Roger. And my attorney will be happy to detail them for you. But the most important reason is a young girl named Mary."

"Who?" he asked, as I'd hoped he would.

I started toward the garage. "Don't move, darling husband. I'll be right back."

'Til next time,

V

"You'll absolutely love V—in fact, you'll wish you were her friend. But since that can't be arranged, you'll happily settle for reading her diary and discovering her most private thoughts and all the outrageous things that happen in her life."

—Kate White, editor-in-chief, *Cosmopolitan*

ALSO BY DEBRA KENT

Diary of V: The Affair

THE DIARY OF

The Breakup

DEBRA KENT

WARNER BOOKS

A Time Warner Company

WARNER BOOKS EDITION

Cover design by Diane Luger

Book design by Stanley S. Drate / Folio Graphics Co., Inc.

Warner Books, Inc.
1271 Avenue of the Americas
New York, NY 10020

Visit our Web site at
www.twbookmark.com

For more information on Time Warner Trade Publishing's online publishing program, visit www.ipublish.com.

 A Time Warner Company

Printed in the United States of America

First Printing: August 2001

10 9 8 7 6 5 4 3 2 1

For Martha Spitzer
and in memory of Chelsea Desdemona

Acknowledgments

This book would not be possible without my agent Sandy Dijkstra, who amazes me with her energy and endurance; Elizabeth James, who works tirelessly but remains astoundingly patient; Amy Applegate, scrupulous and always supportive; my editor Beth de Guzman, whose insights and seamless editing I treasure; Jennifer Woodhouse at Hearst, for her assistance with Valerie Ryan's online adventures; Andy Mallor, for his astute guidance with legal plotlines; Lisa Kamen, for her hilarious stories; Pam Nelson, who is a magician, regardless of the sign on her door; Alisa Sutor, who brought the beach back into my life; Cindy Bailey, who brings sanity to my home.

As always, I owe much to Donna Wilber and Lorraine Rapp for their friendship. I am grateful for the love and support of Adam and Lisi Kent-Isaac and Poe, Joseph P. Kendicott and Coley Coltrane, who inspire me every day. Finally, Valerie's adventures would never have made it to the printed page if not for my most excellent husband, Jeff Isaac.

Dear loyal V fans and new fans alike,

When *Redbook* set out to bring you the fictional *Diary of V* on our Web site, we never knew it would become so successful, with thousands of you logging on each week for your fix of the suburban exploits of Valerie Ryan. V's certainly had her ups and downs, but never so much so as during the spring and summer of 2000, when, on the Web, V faced a life-or-death dilemma, found her husband's secret love shack, and still managed to attend her first Overeaters Anonymous meeting. It was during that time that some fans actually wrote alternative versions on their own Web sites. So we decided to give you here, in the second book of the three-book version of the *Diary of V*, an alternative story line. Consider it a bonus for being such loyal fans. And for new fans, check out the original story line on the *Redbook* Web site, at www.redbook mag.com. Thanks for following V's adventures, and root for her to soldier on—with or without the Prozac!

Sincerely,
Lesley Jane Seymour
Editor in Chief, *Redbook* magazine

Valerie Ryan's marriage is in crisis, her career as a psychotherapist is in shambles, and her libido is as voracious as ever. Over the course of a whirlwind year, Valerie, mother of preschool son Petey, uncovers the pathological infidelity of her playwright/creative writing professor husband, plunges into an affair of her own with the burly Eddie Bennedetto, flirts with the cute but geeky Ben Murphy, and fends off sexual advances from former co-worker Diana Pierce, a randy embezzler and recovering alcoholic. Acting on a tip, Valerie ransacks her house for evidence of husband Roger's infidelity and his alleged fortune. The hidden file she discovers—proof of Roger's disgusting deed—will change her marriage and life forever. But will it force V to abandon all hope of falling in love again?

December 12

My gut clenched as I scanned the file. There was a deed to Plot 9 NE, 144 Lark's Way, Lake Merle Condominium Community. Lark's Way, like something out of a Disney movie, so innocent, so light, a place for yellow shutters and window box geraniums and newlyweds and cartoon birds twittering in delight. How could Roger own a condo—an actual house with a kitchen and carpeting and utility bills—and keep it a secret from me? And why?

I thumbed through the file and found the condo maintenance agreement ($429/mo) and a photocopy of something called "Declaration of Covenants, Restrictions, and Conditions of the Lake Merle Condominium Community." Fifteen pages of rules and regulations: No yard signs. No chain-link fences. No animals or livestock with the exception of dogs, cats, and common household pets. No exterior antennas or satellite dishes. Clotheslines, garbage pails, woodpiles, and other similar items shall be concealed, blah, blah, blah. The last page was signed by Glenn McClintock, president of the Lake Merle Condominium Community. Sally Krauss, notary public. At the bottom of the page was Roger's pretentiously outsized signature. I hurriedly flipped through the papers. I found an envelope filled with pale blue standard-issue check stubs. The checking account was in Roger's name. The checks were made out to the Lake Merle Development Corporation in the amount of $429.

I used to think that my biggest problem was Roger's impulsive affair with a slatternly young protégée. Now I realize that my husband didn't merely have a lover, but another life, another household! I started to hyperventilate. My hands tingled. I felt completely unmoored, and it terrified me.

My mother, who would shoot my husband herself if she possessed the firearms, offered an unusually generous interpretation: Maybe Roger's condo isn't for shacking up. Maybe it's a real estate investment, another secret asset, like the gold bullions Diana claims Roger has hidden somewhere in my house.

'Til next time,

V

December 13

Roger has gone downtown, undoubtedly to replace the magnificent wardrobe I'd destroyed in my rage. I hope he gets hit by a truck. Actually, I hope I get hit by a truck. I can barely drag myself out of bed these days. I feel completely worthless. I have no appetite;

in fact, I've lost four pounds, although four pounds hardly make a difference when you feel like you're fourteen thousand pounds overweight. I'm always on the edge of tears. I cried in the supermarket because I couldn't find Kellogg's corn flake crumbs. They weren't in aisle 9 with the bread crumbs and they weren't in aisle 11 with corn flakes, and after I'd traversed every single stupid row of that stupid store I finally asked the assistant manager and he looked at me like I was speaking in tongues and I felt the tears flood my eyes and I had to turn away.

"You don't understand," I heard myself telling him. "Christmas is only two weeks away, my house is a pig sty, I haven't bought a single present, my ornaments are still sitting in cardboard boxes in the hallway and it'll be Easter by the time I get my lights up. But right now all I care about is making dinner for my little boy, so just tell me where you people are hiding the goddamn corn flake crumbs, okay?"

Everything Roger says and does drives me to the precipice of despair. It doesn't matter whether he's being nice, nasty, or neutral. I hate everything that comes out of his mouth. I hate everything about him. I hate the way he picks his teeth with the edge of a business card. I hate how he adjusts his chiropractically correct pillow so it's just so before going to sleep. I hate how he never replaces the toilet paper but simply stacks a new roll on top of the old cardboard tube. I hate how he snores, how he eats, how he pees in rhythmic spurts. I hate how he always reads the newspaper before I do, then leaves all the pages out of order on the floor of the downstairs bathroom. I hate his smell, his tassled loafers, his hairless chest, his tiny ass.

But most of all, I hate myself. If it weren't for Petey, I'd just kill myself—if I could figure out a way to do it painlessly. I'm too chicken to try to overdose on pills. How would I do it? With four hundred Sudafeds? Even if I had the right pills, what if it didn't work? What if I just wound up paralyzed? Roger would parade his girlfriends past me; they'd shove applesauce into my face and giggle or stick crazy hats on my head and take Polaroid pictures. So I don't think I'll try to kill myself.

'Til next time,

V

December 14

Eddie e-mailed me. He wanted me to meet him at the Roundtree. I told him to forget it. Now I know I'm depressed. The snow has turned to filthy slush. I sobbed my way through *Judge Judy,* a *Matlock* rerun, and *Unsolved Mysteries*. I ate half a roll of frozen Pillsbury chocolate chip cookie dough.

I've got to make two appointments tomorrow, one with a divorce lawyer, Omar Sweet, another with

Holly Wilmack, a psychiatrist at the hospital. I'd referred lots of patients to her, always with good results. I think I'm ready for Prozac. I wonder if she'll agree.

As if I wasn't sufficiently demoralized, I stopped by my parents' house after dropping Pete off at school. My mother had set Dad up in the living room, propped him up on the couch with an afghan across his lap. He looked like a little old lady. There was a metal snack table covered with brown plastic pill bottles. Dad roused himself and tried to smile, but his eyes seemed wild and terrified, like a trapped animal's. He says he doesn't know if it's the chemo or the cancer that's killing him.

I glanced around the room. This year there would be no Christmas tree, no icicle lights along the porch, no wreath on the door, no painted wooden snowman in the foyer.

In the kitchen Mom told me she knew it would be Dad's last Christmas, and she had wanted to make it special, but she didn't have the stamina. I yelled at her for being so negative, then apologized for yelling at her.

I know how awful and selfish this must sound, but as I sat there with him, pretending to watch CNN, all I could think was: I don't need this now. I don't want to think about my father dying now.

Mom suggested I stay home, forget about getting another job. "Take it easy for a change, Val," she said. "Have a little fun. Bake cookies. Redo the basement.

Learn how to use that espresso machine Dad and I bought you for Christmas five years ago." The prospect of living off Roger's trust fund, or, more likely, his alimony checks, seems illicit, tantalizing, exotic. I've worked since I was fifteen years old and never had the nerve to even imagine myself unemployed. A few times I shyly hinted that I might like staying home with Pete, but Roger always reacted with horror and disdain. "You can't be serious," he would snort. "You? Domesticated? That's a laugh." I used to think Roger wanted me in the office because he didn't want to lose the income, but now I know that he simply wanted me out of the house so he could pursue his liaisons.

I think of all the stay-at-home mothers I know, bright and capable women who seem content to live off their husbands' incomes. They insisted they would stay at home until their children started school, then admitted they adored their lives of unencumbered and relatively placid domesticity and had no intention of abandoning it—ever. Carrie Freed was a driven investment counselor. Now she spends her days learning the flute, cultivating African violets, and managing her kids' schedules. When I asked her if it was hard to adjust, she whispered behind her hand, "Are you kidding? I'm having the time of my life." Bonnie Webb-Wilson was an architect in Chicago until her husband was transferred here. She could have found another job, but decided to use the move as her escape hatch from the pressures and demands of a high-powered profession. Now she keeps busy as a room mother and leader of her son's Boy Scout troop.

"You're as busy as ever," I said, challenging her.

"But it's *good* busy," she explained. "I get to spend time with my kid and there's none of that old pressure and panic."

I'm just wondering if any new pressures and panics would pop up if I were to make a similar life change.

'Til next time,

V

December 16

Had a panic attack sitting in Omar Sweet's waiting room. I would have thrown up, but there was nothing in my stomach. All I'd eaten was half a tangerine, and that was last night.

I tried as best as I could to calm myself before Omar came out to greet me. The truth is, he had a sexy voice on the phone, and I suppose that the small part of me that's still alive and sexual hoped he would find me attractive. I slipped a cinnamon Altoid into my mouth and waited. I looked around the office, forcing myself to be "fully present." I literally told myself: I am sitting in the waiting room of my divorce lawyer. *My divorce lawyer.* The man who will guide me through the process of legally terminating my marriage. It's not a fantasy anymore. It's not a spiteful threat I'd toss in Roger's face in an argument. This is for real.

Omar Sweet bounded into the waiting room. He was about fifty, trim, elegant. He was one of those men who surrendered to his balding pate by shaving the rest of his head (I admire that) instead of struggling to arrange sixteen strands of hair. His polished dome gave him a sleek, slightly menacing appearance. He had a graying goatee, sharp white teeth, and aquiline nose. "Ms. Ryan! A pleasure. Please, come in." He gripped my hand firmly and offered a quick smile, and in that moment I knew I'd found the right attorney.

We spent the hour talking about the divorce laws in our state (interesting), his track record (excellent), and his fee structure (expensive). I had a bank check prepared for his retainer ($3,000) and left his office feeling surprisingly more relaxed than when I'd arrived. But by the time I got home, I was dispirited again. I don't know what's depressing me most, that my marriage is ending, or that it's not ending soon enough. Omar urged me to keep up the front until all the facts about Roger's financial holdings have been gathered. He gave me the name of an investigator who, Omar promises, will unearth everything there is to know about Roger in forty-eight hours. I know I should do it, but I'm also afraid to spend any more money.

'Til next time,

𝒱

December 17

Today I went to a baby shower organized by the perpetually neighborly Lynette Kohl-Chase. I didn't know the expectant mom—a young woman named Jennifer Davis—but I welcomed the opportunity to meet some of my neighbors, people I've never seen at any point in the six years I've lived in this house, people I wouldn't recognize if I tripped over them. But, then, why *would* I recognize them? Every morning they roll out of their garages in vans with tinted windows, and every evening they drive back into their garages and close the automatic doors behind them. They don't garden, they don't walk their dogs, they don't walk anywhere. Last year I exchanged phone numbers and addresses with a father of one of Pete's classmates; we were on the same committee and needed to plan a fund-raiser. I looked at his address. He lived on my street. I had never laid eyes on him. The only time I see some of these neighbors is when I go trick-or-treating with Pete, but I've already forgotten what they look like by the following Halloween.

I asked Jennifer what she planned to name the baby. "Trey if it's a boy," she said, "and Lokia if it's a girl."

I thought I'd heard wrong. "Lokia?"

"Yes. My husband and I made it up," she said, smiling proudly. "It's kind of like Loki, the Greek god."

I know I probably shouldn't have said anything, but I couldn't help myself. "Are you totally set on that name?" I began, trying to sound light. "Because, well, you know, lochia is what you call that weird vaginal discharge you get after you give birth. It's pronounced the same way."

"Excuse me?" Jennifer asked.

"No, I mean, I'm just wondering. Also, Loki isn't a Greek god. He's a Norse god. By the way."

Nobody said anything. I left soon afterward.

'Til next time,

V

December 18

I've just taken my first dose of Prozac, half a pill, five milligrams. I can't help feeling defeated, as if I'm taking the easier path. I'm also resentful. If Roger's the jerk, why am I the one on medication? But I also know that I am depressed. I'm not satisfied with my life. I no longer enjoy life's little pleasures. I'm irritable. I feel worn out. I'm not eating (or I'm eating rolls of frozen cookie dough).

Holly says I should begin to feel better in about a month. I'll have to be hopeful, if not for my own sake, then for Petey's. I've seen how depression infects kids in the household.

'Til next time,
𝒱

December 18, continued

I've appropriated half the basement for a small office and I consider this a good sign: I'm considering starting a private practice from the house! I bought an iMac, printer, scanner, and small computer desk, a cordless phone, halogen lamp, and a clock radio. I checked the classifieds and found a used copy machine for only seventy-five bucks! The woman who sold it to me—the office manager at A-1 Realty—assured me it worked perfectly. Roger was poised to give me grief about spending the money, but I deadpanned that I wanted to work from home "so I can be closer to you, my darling." He squinted at me suspiciously but kept his mouth shut.

'Til next time,
𝒱

December 22

I've spent the last few days trying to get in touch with my inner Martha. I've finished decorating the tree, hung the lights, made Christmas lanterns from gourds, created an enormous fresh fir wreath for the front door, scrubbed out the parakeet's cage, reorganized the pantry, pulled out my old sewing machine, and made Pete a big red sock to hang over the fireplace.

'Til next time,
V

December 27

Roger has made it clear that he wants to have sex tonight. He arranged for Petey to have a sleep over. He announced that he's making grilled salmon and fresh bread and my favorite salad (spinach, chilled asparagus, goat cheese, and raspberry vinaigrette). He cleaned the house. This is Roger at his most romantic. I couldn't be less interested. What the hell am I going to do?

'Til next time,
V

December 27, continued

As I'd expected, Roger had orchestrated the entire evening as a prelude to sex. He came up behind me as I rinsed dishes in the sink, and I felt nothing but revulsion and an urge to squirt dishwashing liquid in his eyes. But I lolled my head back and let him press against me. He plunged his hands into the soapy water, resting them over mine as I sponged the dishes, and it reminded me of that sexy scene in *Ghost* where Patrick Swayze and Demi Moore play with the clay on the pottery wheel. Except that Roger wasn't Patrick Swayze, I wasn't Demi Moore, we weren't in love, and it didn't feel sexy, but wet and disgusting. I stared at the bits of asparagus and gray salmon skin floating in the water and felt dinner inch its way back up my esophagus. I tried not to gag as Roger kissed the nape of my neck.

While Roger licked my neck, I pictured the condo on Lake Merle. It was probably one of those woodsy developments, pretty cedar units nestled into the trees. I bitterly remembered the times I'd suggested buying a summer place on Lake Merle. I thought it would be the ideal weekend retreat. I wanted to get a little boat and teach Pete to sail. "Buy a place an hour away from home? What kind of vacation is that?" he'd sneer. "Besides, the lake's polluted anyway. PCBs. That factory in Windsor." All that time, he owned a condo right there on the supposedly polluted lake. A condo we could have enjoyed as a family. I wanted to scream.

Roger pulled my hands out of the water and patted them gently with the dish towel and raised them to his mouth. "This can wait," he said, sucking my fingers, one by one. "Let's go upstairs." As he led me up the steps, my mind desperately searched for a plausible excuse. I could say I had a stomach flu, or a migraine. But then he might suspect something. Roger knew I was usually ready for sex. Even when I was mad at him for coming home late, or coming home drunk—even in the midst of the Alyssa affair—I'd rarely pass up an opportunity to have sex. I'd never understood women who wouldn't have sex unless everything was absolutely perfect: They had to be happy. They had to be in love. They had to be in the mood. They had to be romanced. Sex wasn't about sex, it was about emotional attachment. Two hearts beating as one. As far as I was concerned, love and romance were nice but not necessary. Sex was a biological function, a release, an explosion of pleasure. As soon as you start putting conditions on sex, as soon as you start intellectualizing it, you've ruined it.

Tonight my philosophy was put to the test. First came the strawberry massage oil. He licked me from my toes to my eyelids, spending a good ten minutes in between—utterly nauseating. When he finally began thrusting inside me, I felt nothing but rage. I clawed his back and bit his shoulder, which he naturally interpreted as animal lust. "Oooh, baby," he groaned. "You're wild tonight." He never knew it was hate, not lust, that made me want to tear his flesh away. When he climaxed, I started to sob. He stayed inside me and whispered, "Oh, sweetheart." He rolled off me and reached for my hand. "That was incredible." He kissed my hand. "You are incredible, you know that? A beast!"

"No, Roger, you're the beast," I told him.

"I guess I am. But you inspire me." He propped himself up on an elbow. "You know, I think this was like a new beginning for us, don't you?" I made some kind of noncommittal noise—*hmmm*—and he went on. "We can put everything behind us. Just sweep it out the door. Start fresh. New year, new marriage!" I made more vague noises. I knew if I waited long enough, he'd fall asleep. In three minutes Roger was snoring like an asthmatic pig. I slid out of bed and used Pete's bathroom to shower off his stink. Then I went downstairs to watch CNN.

'Til next time,

𝒱

December 28

Roger wanted to have sex again this morning but Pete came home early so Roger went shopping for more clothes. In the meantime, I attacked the file cabinets in the basement but found nothing useful. Pete had a friend over, a neighborhood boy with the cruelly incongruous name Hunter. Despite the macho appellation, the child is afraid of everything, including the parakeet. Pete pulled out his Pokémon cards, Wishbone videos, puzzles, checkers, Lincoln Logs—anything to engage this child. The boy was an amoeba! He wouldn't play with anything, I invited Hunter only so Pete could have someone to distract him while I searched Roger's files. I felt guilty. They would have more fun if I'd taken the time to guide them. When Pete went over to Hunter's house, he always returned home with some crafty little thing. They made picture frames out of twigs and twine, Christmas trees from pine cones. Hunter's mother, Lynette Kohl-Chase, created topiaries and elaborate family scrapbooks and mosaic bird baths. She had hand-painted all the tiles in her kitchen, thirty-eight of which were decorated with farm animals in a kind of French provincial style she copied detail for detail from a home decorating magazine.

She made me want to retch.

'Til next time,

V

December 29

Since I neglected Petey yesterday, I made it up to him tonight by playing something like seventy-two rounds of Candy Land before bed. Eventually I had to stack the deck just to end the game; I made sure Petey had Snowflake Queen Frostine and prayed neither of us would get stuck in Molasses Swamp or lost in Lollipop Woods. After I'd finally gotten Pete settled for the night, I accidentally stepped on the game box and flattened it, and Pete started screaming and hurling his pillows to the floor. I know he was over-tired and probably pissed off at Hunter, but the tantrum scared me. I'd never seen him so angry over something so minor. Now I've got to tape up the corners of the box, and I have no idea where I put the masking tape. My house is a friggin' mess. Oh, crap.

'Til next time,
V

December 30

Still on Prozac, still no change, except for a weird taste in my mouth, and a slightly nauseous feeling—which actually isn't such a bad thing if it helps me lose weight. I know that some people gain weight on this medication. Maybe I'll be one of the lucky ones who actually loses a few pounds!

Martha Stewart be damned, I ordered pizza for dinner. Too tired to cook. Ran out to my parents' house. Pete wanted to come, but I made him stay home with Roger. I don't think either of my parents could handle having him tearing around the house right now.

Started hunting for the gold bullions while Roger was asleep. Poked around behind some ceiling tiles in the basement. Nada.

'Til next time,
V

January 4

I am going to hire Omar's investigator. I am sick of playing Sherlock. I don't even know what I'm looking for.

I called the number Omar had given me. L.T. Investigative Services. I pictured a paunchy guy in a short-sleeved dress shirt. L.T. turned out to be Libby Taylor. She sounded young enough to be one of my baby-sitters. At first she said she couldn't see me until next week, and my heart sank, but her secretary Dave mentioned a last-minute cancellation. She asked if I could be there in twenty minutes. Her office was on the south side of town. I knew a shortcut. I made it in a ten.

Libby Taylor, P.I., looked only a little older than she'd sounded. She was wearing jeans, hiking boots, and a bright red Old Navy sweatshirt. She was shorter than me. She had the kind of naturally curly hair that needed nothing more than a quick towel-dry in the morning, and features that required no cosmetic enhancement. Clear skin, almond-shaped brown eyes, small bow lips. Libby offered me a cup of green tea and a chocolate chip cookie. I felt comfortable with her but her youth made me nervous.

Libby saw me eyeing her diploma, a law degree from Yale. "Both my parents are lawyers, and, frankly, they're both miserable, whether or not they're willing to admit it," she said. She bit into a cookie. "I always wanted to be an investigator. I'm good at it, and I enjoy it. Studying law wasn't a total waste. Comes in handy on the job. And people seem to be impressed by the diploma." She seems to have a good track record. She gets steady referrals from the top six corporate and family law firms in the state. She's worked on everything from extramarital affairs to insurance fraud, but her specialty is digging up buried assets.

"How do you feel about digging up buried gold?" I asked her.

She laughed. "Aye-aye-matey. If you've got the treasure map, I'll bring the shovel. But I'm afraid I don't have a parrot."

"No, I'm serious. I have reason to believe that my husband has gold hidden somewhere in the house. Bullions."

"Then we'll find it." Libby wasn't smiling anymore. I told her about Roger's affair with Alyssa, about Diana's allegations, about the hidden file I'd found in the basement. Libby listened attentively, asked a few pointed questions, and typed notes into a laptop. Her young face was compassionate, earnest. "Your husband did you wrong, Ms. Ryan. And I have no intention of letting him off the hook." She stood up, a signal that our meeting was over. "I'll send you a letter with a game plan and my fee schedule. Take a day to look it over, and we'll talk again."

She extended her small hand and gripped mine confidently. "I'm so glad you chose to speak with me."

On the way out I met Dave the secretary, who must have been in the bathroom when I'd arrived. He was a magnificent creature in a body-hugging black ribbed sweater and snug black jeans. "Have a great day, ma'am," he called out. How I hated that word. I don't care if it's supposed to be a sign of respect. It was dowdy as a housedress and I refused to wear it.

'Til next time,

V

January 5

I went online and ordered this special cream designed to plump up lips. I read all about it in one of those celebrity style magazines. Apparently all these beautiful actresses use it to keep their lips looking young and juicy. It was forty dollars for a tube the size of a Polly Pocket but it'll be worth every penny if it works.

'Til next time,

V

January 9

My new computer is too slow. And I think the lady at A-1 Realty lied to me. The copy machine doesn't work.

'Til next time,

V

January 10

I got two estimates to repair the copier. Lakeland Office Supply said it would cost $280. Executive Business Machines would fix it for $295.50. That's like four times more than I paid for the machine. Then I remembered Kevin, the sweet guy who handled most of the repairs at my old workplace—he fixed fax machines, copiers, computers, you name it. He even fixed one of the toilets after someone (I say it was my former boss Cadence) tried to flush down a sanitary napkin. Kevin is fast and cheap and he guarantees his work. He's rather cute in a scholarly way, as I recall. But how would I locate him? I never knew his last name. He was always Kevin-the-repair-guy.

I phoned Filomena, the receptionist at the Center, who told me in her characteristically world-weary way that she had been promoted to office manager. She gave me Kevin's number and I wished her well. It wasn't until after I hung up that I realized my hands were shaking. Calling the Center was like making contact with a ghost. Or, more accurately, making contact with the living. Filomena was in a world of movement, growth, and adult conversation, a world of elevators and proposals and new clients and business lunches. I was the dead one now.

'Til next time,

V

January 11

The lip-plumping cream arrived today! It smells like oranges and coconut. I can feel it working already!

'Til next time,

V

January 12

Now I feel really guilty. Petey begged me to invite over Hunter-the-Blob again. I dialed the number and handed Pete the phone; I wanted to avoid talking to the ever perky Lynette, didn't want to hear how she was sponge-painting the basement. After a few moments, Pete waved the receiver at me. "Hunter's mom wants to talk to you."

I took the phone from Petey and tried to sound cheerful. "Hi, Lynette," I said, fake-breezily. "I guess the boys are cooking up a plan, huh?"

"I don't think this is going to work," she said. Her voice sounded uncharacteristically tight. Something was wrong.

"Oh?" I said, trying to stay calm. "Why not?"

"Valerie, I'll be honest. Whenever Hunter comes back from your house, well, he's always a little off-the-wall. Do you know what I mean?"

I pictured Hunger vegetating on my sofa. Is that what passes for off-the-wall in the Kohl-Chase household? "Really? Tell me more," I said, trying to sound like the caring-yet-detached therapist I used to be, instead of the hysterical, guilt-stricken mother I am now.

"I don't know how to say this, Valerie, but it's my impression that the boys just aren't properly supervised." I bit my lip and waited. "Did you know, for instance, that they played with matches in your backyard last week?"

"What? No! Of course I didn't know! Are you sure?" I knew she was sure. Lynette Kohl-Chase was always sure.

"Apparently they were trying to build a campfire." She paused. "And did you know they tried to carve boats out of Ivory soap using steak knives?" I suddenly remembered seeing scraps of soap on the kitchen floor. I hadn't given it a second thought—just another piece of crap on my floor, what else was new? Now I felt like disemboweling myself. Pete goes to her house, and they build gingerbread houses. Hunter comes here, and they play with steak knives and matches. What could I say? I was a horrible, neglectful, pitiful excuse for a mother and we both knew it.

"No offense," Lynette went on, "but I think it's best if Hunter stays home today." She paused. "Of course, Pete is always welcome here. In fact, we're building an igloo on the deck if he's interested."

I wanted to say, Oh shut the hell up, Mrs. Perfect-Mother-and-Homemaker-Who-Makes-Me-Want-to-

Hurl-My-Guts-Out. Instead I told her Pete would rather stay here. "We're making double-chocolate brownies," I lied. "From scratch. Pete's favorite."

"Oh, that's lovely," Lynette chirped. "Maybe some other time." I'm sure she knew I was lying. I'm sure of it.

'Til next time,

V

January 13

I woke up this morning with a rash around my mouth. It looks like I have a mustache of red pimples. It itches, and it's hideous, and I feel like crying. I guess my new lip plumper worked, though tumescent is probably a better word to describe what has happened to the lower part of my face.

As I sit here with hydrocortizone cream slathered all over my face, I'm thinking about what it will be like to be single and alone again, and I'm afraid. The trauma of Roger's infidelity has left me feeling battered and shaky. I feel so unsure of myself, my worth, my looks. I don't know if I have the stamina to put myself "on the market." Years without love have made me feel unlovable. While I cognitively understand that Roger is a sick bastard, at the visceral level, I can't help but believe I deserved him. I am plagued by the fear that I'm literally incapable of choosing a good man, or that no good man would want me. In darker moments, I convince myself that no normal man would want a woman my age whose body has born a child, whose belly is striped with faded stretch marks, and whose breasts sag like water balloons. It's like the real estate market in the suburbs. Why would anyone want to buy one of the 1960s bi-levels when they can get a shiny, new house in a shiny, new subdivision? The old houses sit on the market like relics from another age.

There's Eddie, I guess. But he's not exactly the marrying kind, and not just because he's already married. Eddie is my first affair, my secret sin, my co-conspirator. One day he will be my former lover, but he can never be my future second husband.

'Til next time,

V

January 14

It's 5 A.M. and I'm sitting here wondering how I missed the clues. Why hadn't I paid attention? Why hadn't I picked up on the signs? Before Roger and I got married, I struggled with a cancerous jealousy. But I desperately wanted to be a trusting wife. In therapy, I learned to view my suspicions as infantile impulses, irrational longings that had more to do with childhood wounds than my fiancé's wandering eye. Instead of stiffening when Roger mentioned a woman's name, I eventually learned to relax. I welcomed many of those women into my home, served them dinner, laughed with them, trusted them. *I was such a sucker!*

I suppose that Roger's sudden interest in expensive clothes was one sign, though I didn't realize it at the time. And the introduction of new sexual positions. Then there was the female rapper sex music— once I borrowed his van and when I turned the key in the ignition, hip-hop music boomed at full blast: "I like it hard and thick and I like to lick/I like it in my butt and I like to strut . . ." At first I thought it was the radio, then I realized it was a CD. I found the case under the seat. It showed three busty girls in sequinned thongs. I couldn't believe Roger was listening to this kind of music. He thought Snoop Doggy Dog was a cartoon character. I guess I should have paid attention.

'Til next time,

V

January 15

In my ongoing effort to appear normal, I agreed to go with Roger to Starbucks last night, to meet Wade and Melanie Rosen, a couple I've known for years and always enjoy, but rarely see since they started raising race horses two years ago. Wade is a lovable panda, and Mel has a bizarre sense of humor—she once joked about starting a company that did theme funerals. "You know, we could do a luau funeral. Or a Mexican fiesta funeral. Our slogan would be, 'We put the *fun* in *funerals.*' Get it?"

After eleven (childless, I feel compelled to point out) years of marriage, Mel and Wade are still wildly in love. If I didn't like them so much, I'd hate them. In fact, I might kill them. After I killed Lynette Kohl-Chase. "Hey! Have you checked out Paradise Suites?" Mel asked, dipping a tongue into her latte. My throat tightened. As far as the Rosens were concerned, Roger and I were stable and happy, and I wasn't about to disabuse them of that notion.

"No! Tell us!" I said, faking interest. This couple's vigorous sex life was the last thing I wanted to talk about.

"Oh! You guys! You've got to try this place," Wade chimed in. He was stroking his wife's curly brown hair. "Mirrors everywhere. Free dirty movies. And a hot tub to die for. Shaped like a heart."

"So's the bed. A great big heart!" Melanie exclaimed. "What a weekend! I think I lost ten pounds from all the exercise!"

Wade ran a hand over his wife's plump belly. "You're gorgeous, with or without the ten pounds."

Melanie tittered. "I may be chubby, but I can sure please my hubby!" The next thing you know, they're making out. I wanted to cry. Here I am, sitting there with my future former husband, while this sweet, rotund, deliriously happy couple necked like teenagers. They weren't just lovers, they were best friends. I pictured them sitting on twin rocking chairs on the nursing home porch. She was his little hotsy-totsy. I WANTED TO BE SOMEONE'S HOTSY TOTSY, DAMN IT! Wade grabbed his wife's cheek and said, "Isn't she a doll? Don't you want to eat her up?"

"Actually, we should probably leave that task to you, Wade," Roger said, droll as ever. I despised him.

As we were leaving I thought I saw someone watching me from the corner table. Ben Murphy. He smiled brightly and waved. I waved back, perhaps a bit too wistfully. Then I felt something slide down my pant leg. I looked down. It was black, it was soft. At first I thought, absurdly, Oh! It's a black kitten. A black kitten was hiding in my pants leg! Then I realized it wasn't a kitten, it was my bunched-up black underwear, the underwear I wore yesterday, the underwear I forgot to disengage from my pants when I put them on again this morning. I quickly scooped up the panties and shoved them in my bag. Ben didn't notice. Wade and Melanie didn't notice. But Roger noticed. He rolled his eyes and shook his head as if to say, "You poor, pathetic slob." And even if he wasn't thinking it, I was.

'Til next time,

V

January 16

The Prozac must finally be taking effect, because I'm feeling strangely detached from everyone and everything. When I returned home from the health club last night, I found Roger watching the basketball game. Dishes were stacked in the sink, and Pete—who should have been in bed—was sitting on the kitchen floor in his Pokémon underwear eating Cocoa Puffs out of the box.

This in itself is nothing new. Once basketball season commences, everything else can go to hell as far as Roger's concerned. What *is* new: I didn't really care! Sure, it all registered when I walked in: Pete. Awake. Underwear. Cocoa Puffs. The thing is, I didn't feel *anything*, as if I'd been anesthetized, which sounds unpleasant, but is exactly what I've needed. For once, I had no interest in arguing with Roger. I just led Pete upstairs, tucked him in, jumped into the shower, and went to bed.

'Til next time,

V

January 17

Libby Taylor's letter came this morning. Her fee is $250 a day. She said she'd have the job completed in ten to twelve business days. She wanted $500 now, and the balance after she turned in her report. I called and gave her the go-ahead. Now comes the hard part. Waiting.

'Til next time,

V

January 18

Yay! Keven is a genius. He fixed my copy machine. Total cost: sixty-five dollars and he threw in an extra toner cartridge. He also told me he could upgrade my computer so it would run programs like Napster. I invited him to stay for a cup of coffee and he agreed without hesitation. I hinted at the deteriorating state of my marriage, and he admitted to a string of unhappy relationships with women. I noticed he was wearing a Michigan sweatshirt. I probed a little and found out that he dropped out of Michigan in his senior year—he was a philosophy major—and never finished his degree. He wouldn't say why. He'd always had a knack for building and fixing things, so he went into business for himself. "I still read philosophy," he said mildly. I refilled his cup. "It's a hobby, I guess." I noticed that his eyes were the loveliest hue, a golden brown, like amber. I thought I could lose myself in those eyes. It was so nice to have a man in the house.

As we spoke, amidst his high-tech clutter, with the sunlight streaming through the blinds, I watched his smooth hands circle the coffee cup. He seemed like a man with secrets, a man who nursed some deep and tragic wound, and while this should have repelled me, I found it intensely attractive. I wondered what his secret might be.

Eddie called to insist that there's no reason to wait for Libby's report. He wants to come over and help me search the house. Pete has a Tiger Cub pow-wow this weekend at Wesley Woods, and Roger is supposedly attending a writers' retreat. I told Eddie he could stop by Saturday, around noon. I suspect he has more on his mind than gold.

'Til next time,

𝒱

January 21

Eddie and I spent all afternoon and most of the evening searching for Roger's hidden stash of gold bullions. We removed the ceiling tiles in the basement: nothing. Using a metal detector and stud finder, we scanned the drywall and floorboards: nothing. We looked behind the circuit breaker box in the garage: nothing. We pawed through every drawer in every dresser and cabinet in the house, through every box in the basement and garage, through every shelf and shoebox in every closet. No gold. I'm beginning to suspect Diana fabricated everything.

I did, however, find the missing Austrian crystal necklace my father gave me on my sixteenth birthday, my Miles Davis CD, the power drill chuck key, a Norton Utilities disk, Pete's preschool class picture, and my favorite leather gloves. We also found Roger's stack of *Hustler* magazines. Six years' worth. If these had been my husband's only deep, dark secret, I would have been stunned. But compared to everything else I now know about the man, I just shook my head and laughed.

As I write this, Eddie is sleeping on the couch. Despite my recent exhortations on the joys of unencumbered sex, I wasn't in the mood tonight. I should be able to screw with impunity now. I've got nothing to lose. But I couldn't locate even the tendrils of arousal. Maybe it's the Prozac, or maybe it's the fact that Eddie started to look a bit too *comfortable* in my house, walking around in his underwear and drinking orange juice straight from the carton. He seemed settled. I wanted him to go away. When he started tugging at my clothes, I suggested he go back to his wife.

"I can't," he said. "I'm supposed to be in Chicago. At a convention."

"Plant guys have conventions?"

Then the phone rang. "Put my husband on," said the voice on the other end. I froze. "Look, I know he's there. Just put him on."

What was I supposed to tell her? That her husband couldn't come to the phone because he was busy convincing me to go to bed with him? "I'm sorry. Who's this?" I said, stalling. I could hear kids shrieking in the background.

"Don't bullshit me, Mrs. Ryan," she snarled. "I saw his truck in your driveway, okay? Now put my husband on the phone." She was talking loud enough for Eddie to hear. He pantomimed wildly: *No. I'm not here. Tell her I'm not here.*

I hung up on her. Then I pulled the phone off the cradle and listened as the dial tone changed to a nagging beep and then to a grating alert signal, and then, mercifully, to silence.

Eddie walked his fingers up my arm, and along my chest. "Come on, Val." He winked at me. "We could always make believe we're in Chicago at a convention. I'll be the horny conventioneer and you can be room service." Eddie looked warm and delectably rumpled in his flannel boxers; a quick romp on the couch could have been a welcome distraction. He pulled me toward him and kissed me on the mouth, lightly at first, then harder. His hand tightly clenched the back of my neck. I tried to pull away but he held on more tightly. I was having trouble breathing. "Let up a little," I whispered. "No," he grunted. Now he had me against the wall. It scared me. I had a sudden recollection of the time I'd impulsively adopted a sleek, stray German Shepherd from the pound. Alone with the dog in my empty apartment, I saw a surliness in his eyes, a look I hadn't noticed when I'd picked him out. I slept with my bedroom door locked that night and returned him to the pound the following day.

"I guess you're not in the mood," Eddie said finally, wiping his mouth with the back of his hand. And there, in Eddie's eyes, I saw that same surliness.

"It's been a hell of a day, Eddie," I told him. "I'm sure you understand." I heard my voice quaver.

He shrugged his shoulders and grabbed the TV remote. "Whatever."

'Til next time,

V

January 22

Eddie was gone by the time I woke up, and I knew it was over between us. I'm relieved. Happy, actually. Is that me or the Prozac? Is there even a distinction between the two anymore?

When I went to retrieve Pete at Wesley Woods, I found him sitting on his duffel bag outside the cabin. His right hand was wrapped in bandages. It looked like a big white lollipop. Apparently he'd scalded himself on a hot metal pot. After that, he couldn't do much of anything for the rest of the weekend.

I went into the cabin in search of someone in authority. I found Lynette Kohl-Chase, who just happens to be the new assistant cubmaster. She was in full Cub Scout regalia, the dull khaki shirt and plaid neckerchief knotted tightly at her throat, the navy blue cap and matching navy pants, the kind bus drivers wear.

"Why didn't you try to reach me?" I demanded.

"We did," Lynette answered, scanning her clipboard. "At 7:00, at 7:03, at 7:05, at 7:07, at 7:10. The line was busy." She looked at me. "Troop regulations require us to keep a log of all emergency phone calls, and believe me, this was an emergency. Pete was in agony. We continued to try you all night."

I almost collapsed when I remembered that I'd taken the phone off the hook after Eddie's wife called. I can't begin to describe the guilt and heartbreak I felt then, and still feel. "Poor sweetheart," she continued. "We made s'mores. He could barely pick them up with his bandaged hand." I looked into Lynette's clean, earnest face. I wanted to strangle her with that stupid plaid neckerchief.

I buckled Pete into the Jeep and popped in the *Annie* sound track, hoping to lighten the mood. He glared at me in the rearview mirror. "Why didn't you answer the phone?" he asked.

I wanted to cry. "Oh, honey, I didn't know you were trying to call me. I accidentally knocked the phone off the hook. It was off the hook all night. I'm so sorry."

He just stared out the window. I wanted to stamp

it across my forehead: World's Worst Mother. Pete's face was stern, like an old man's. At that moment I sent up a promise to God, a promise to live a cleaner, purer life. I made a mental note to call Reverend Lee.

'Til next time,

V

January 23

Roger called to say he has extended his stay at the writers' retreat. He won't get back until Saturday. Yippee!

Interesting side effect of the Prozac; I can't stop yawning! Big, jaw-cracking yawns. I can't stop myself. The other side effect is gas. Lovely. I stopped by my parents' house, and my father, who slept through most of my visit, woke up long enough to accuse my mother of farting.

I didn't feel obligated to confess, and my mother refused to accept responsibility. Dad started cracking up and said, "She who denied it supplied it." It was so gratifying to see him laugh like that, but he quickly tired himself out and was soon fast asleep again.

In the kitchen, I admitted that I was the culprit, and told her about the Prozac. She was clearly disappointed. "You don't need pills," she said. "You just need a divorce."

"But I'm miserable," I told her.

"Of course you're miserable," she responded. "Who wouldn't be, married to that creep?" Then she started speechifying: Life is supposed to be hard, there are no quick fixes, drugs are bad. I'd heard it all before and wasn't in the mood to hear it again.

"I gotta go, Mom," I told her. I gave her a hug. "Kiss Dad for me when he wakes up, okay?"

She grabbed my hand and squeezed it. "I will." Then she whispered, "No more pills, you hear?" I just shook my head and left.

'Til next time,
V

January 24

Last night I dreamed that Libby Taylor's report came in the mail. It looked like my Visa statement, page after page of charges. On the last page it said, Debit: $649,000. Roger was destitute. Instead of the million-dollar settlement I'd expected, I actually owed the IRS $649,000! I woke up crying. I switched on the light and ran to the bathroom and stared at myself in the mirror. I forced myself to say aloud, "It was a dream." But I never went back to sleep.

'Til next time,
V

January 25

It's amazing, really. The things I used to ruminate about—how Pete's going to handle the divorce, how I'll survive being single—now just pass through my head. It's like transcendental meditation. I notice the thoughts, but I don't fixate on them. I have decided to ignore my mother's anti-Prozac admonitions: Westerners are the only people who seek to avoid suffering. Other cultures accept pain as a normal part of life, but Americans have this crazy idea that we ought to be happy all the time.

So what's wrong with wanting to be happy? What makes this American notion less valid than any other notion about happiness? I say, why not take a cultural relativist approach to the question of happiness: Some cultures seek to accept it, others seek to avoid it, nobody's right and nobody's wrong. It's all cultural, and it's all relative.

Now I may finally have a 20-milligram tool to help me feel some measure of happiness, and I'll be damned if I'm not going to try it.

'Til next time,

V

January 27

Our parakeet died. I found him facedown in the cage. Pete cried until he threw up, a reaction that surprised me given the fact he didn't seem to like the bird. Pete demanded a formal burial. It's been unseasonably warm, and some of the yard was almost swampy after all the rain, so I told him to find the spade in the garage and we'd dig a little grave by the blue spruce. The ground turned out to be harder than I'd expected, and I was ready to abandon the project, but Pete started bawling, so I forged ahead.

Lynette, who apparently starts with a fresh font of goodwill every day while I continue nursing my grudges against her, spied me from her deck. "Aw, did the birdie die?"

Pete nodded mournfully, wiped away a tear with his bandaged lollipop hand.

"Can I help? We've got a fence post digger. Works like a charm. Even on frozen ground." The next thing I knew, Lynette was at my side with her contraption, drilling away.

We all heard it: *Clang!*

"Darn it!" Lynette said. "We must have hit a rock."

We peered into the hole. I tried to stop Lynette from reaching in, but it was too late.

"What the heck is this?" Lynette was bending over the hole. "Oh dear. I hope it's not another little coffin. This isn't some kind of pet cemetery, is it?"

"No. Definitely not," I answered. The bird had been our first real pet. Roger had never allowed animals in the house. He claimed to be allergic, but I eventually realized that he was fearful. When Pete brought home the class gerbil from preschool for the weekend, Roger insisted we keep it in the garage, where it died of hypothermia.

We did have a goldfish once, won it at the county fair. It died the same day, as soon as we transferred it from the Baggie to a real fishbowl. Pete insisted on burying it. Roger sent Pete to bed, promising that he'd put the fish in an Altoids tin and bury it under the blue spruce. I found the fish the next morning, floating in the basement toilet. Apparently Roger had forgotten how unreliable that basement toilet could be. Now I knew that Roger had indeed buried something under the blue spruce, but it wasn't a dead goldfish in an Altoids tin.

Lynette dropped to her knees and stuck a gloved hand into the hole. "Jeez, this thing is heavy," she said, grunting as she pulled something out of the clay soil. It was a strongbox.

"Oh, why don't you just leave it there?" I suggested uneasily.

She looked at me, bewildered. "Are you kidding?" She wiped the hair out of her eyes. "Aren't you curious?"

Pete started hopping up and down. "Maybe it's buried treasure!"

I tried to be cool. "Oh, wait a minute. Now I remember." Pete and Lynette looked at me expectantly while my brain scrambled to fabricate something believable. "I think that must be Roger's time capsule.

You know, for all that millennium business. I'm sure that's what it is."

Lynette scrunched up her face. She was one of the few women who hadn't been charmed by my husband. "Too heavy to be a time capsule." She pulled off her gloves and jammed a manicured finger against the latch. It was locked.

"Dang," she said, scowling. Pete said something like, "You could use my key." I figured he was talking about the key to this little plastic locker my parents gave him for Christmas.

"I don't think that would work, sweetie, but thank you so much for offering," I told him. "You're such a good helper!"

I pulled the box from Lynette's grip. It *was* heavy. Dense, dead weight. It occurred to me that Lynette might think Roger had buried something really scandalous, like drugs or body parts. But I wasn't about to defend his reputation. "Well, Lynette, I might as well take this in. I'm sure Roger wouldn't want us messing with it."

My heart thrummed as I lugged the box up the deck stairs and into the house. I put it on the floor in the family room and tried to pick the lock with everything I could get my hands on. An old luggage key. A bobby pin. A safety pin. The thing you use to pick walnut meat out of the shell. A shishkabob skewer. A screwdriver. I got hotter, sweatier, and more desperate with every attempt. Suddenly, Pete appeared, dangling a key from his good hand. "Try this key, Mommy," he urged.

As he brought it closer, I realized it was not, as I'd assumed, the key to his little plastic locker. This was marked with a Durabox logo, the same imprint on the top of the strongbox. "Where did you get this?" I asked him, trying to appear casual.

Pete looked down and started sucking his thumb, something he hadn't done since he was three. And he had the guiltiest expression on his face. "What is it, sweetie?" I pulled him to my lap. "You can tell me. I promise I won't get mad."

"Daddy put it in my piggy bank," he said. "He thought I was sleeping."

I shoved the little key into the box and turned it. The latch flipped open. And there they were. Stacks of them, like thick Golden Graham crackers, all of them identical in shape and size. I quickly counted the flat bars. There were exactly sixty.

"What are they, Mommy?" Pete asked, staring.

"I'm not sure," I lied. "I think it might be for a printing press or something. Or maybe they're paperweights. Something like that." I snapped the lid shut and tried to distract him. "How would you like to watch a little TV? I think *Rugrats* is on Nick. I'll make popcorn. Okay?"

I grabbed the remote and switched on the set. My hand was shaking. "Want some popcorn?" I felt light-headed. I'd found the gold! I had no idea what those things were worth, but I intended to find out. The banks were closed. I found the phone number for All That Glitters, a jewelry store in the mall. I asked for the going price of gold.

"What have you got? Coins?"

"No, not coins." I realized I didn't even know what these things were called. "You know, flat things." I grabbed a flat bag of microwave popcorn and kneaded the kernels and congealed fake butter with my fingers. I tossed it in the microwave and slammed the door shut.

"Oh, ingots, Five- or ten-ounce?"

I remembered my old Weight Watchers scale in the cabinet above the toaster and pulled it down. "Five ounces. Exactly."

"Okay. Well, gold's up at about $310 an ounce. So you're looking at about $1500 per ingot. Give or take."

I had sixty of them. I did the math. Jesus.

'Til next time,

V

January 28

I slept with my hand on the strongbox. Pete wanted to go to Eggbert's for waffles, but I didn't feel comfortable leaving the gold in the house. I decided that my parents' house was the safest place to stow it. We swung by on the way into town. My mother, ever the Girl Scout, asked me if I might be somehow breaking the law. "After all," she intoned, "it doesn't belong to you."

"Well, Mother, I have no idea who this belongs to. For all I know some pirate buried it there. It's on my property. And until someone tells me otherwise, it's mine."

She grimaced. "If you say so." End of conversation.

'Til next time,

$\mathcal{V}$

January 31

So we're eating dinner, when the phone rings. I check Caller ID. It was Eddie, calling from the office. Against my better judgment, I picked up the phone.

"Sorry about last weekend," he said.

"Hi, Eddie."

"I don't know what got into me," he said. "I guess I got carried away."

"Yes, you did," I told him. I decided not to confess that he'd frightened me. "It wasn't a lot of fun for me." God, that sounded lame, like I was talking to a preschooler. "Pete and I are just finishing up dinner. So I'd better go."

"Hey," he interrupted. "I hope Roger won't mind. I took one of his *Hustler* magazines with me."

"That's fine, Eddie."

"I mean, if I couldn't have you that night, the magazine was the next best thing, if you know what I mean."

I felt my stomach lurch. I wanted to tell him to leave me alone, but I didn't want to make him angry. "That's sweet, Eddie." Sweet?!

"So. Did you find it?"

"No, not yet," I told him. "I think it was all a cock-and-bull story Diana made up just to drive me crazy."

"Say that again," Eddie whispered.

"Say what?"

"You know. Cock and bull."

I felt my face flush. "Please, Eddie. Not now."

He chuckled. "Okay. Later, then."

Something had shifted between Eddie and me. The more I tried to pull away, the more he seemed to want me. I hoped that he wouldn't call again that night, and he didn't.

'Til next time,

V

February 2

Just as I was leaving to pick up Pete, the phone rang. I checked Caller ID. Anonymous. I was afraid it might be Eddie and decided not to pick up. But then I heard a woman's voice—a message. It was Libby

Taylor, the P.I. I quickly picked up the phone before she could hang up. "Yes! I'm here!" I couldn't wait to tell her about the gold. "I've got something to tell you!"

"And *I've* got something to tell *you*, Ms. Ryan." She sounded serious.

"You first," I told her.

"I'm just about done with my investigation of Mr. Tisdale," she began. "Obviously I'll be sending you the full report. But I thought you'd want me to call you first."

"Yes?" I had no idea whether this would be good news or bad.

"Are you sitting down?" she asked. "Because if you're not, I highly recommend you do.

"Based on preliminary calculations, your husband's net worth—investments, stocks, bonds, mutual funds, the Swiss accounts, the money in the Caymans, real estate holdings, the art—"

I cut her off. "Art?"

"Yes. A Caravaggio sketch and Roy Lichtenstein canvas. He keeps them at his parents' house. You've never noticed them?"

"I thought they were prints."

"At any rate, you're looking at a net worth of $82 million, give or take a few hundred thousand." She gave me a moment to absorb the information. My eyeballs were buzzing. I felt giddy and hot.

"Ms. Ryan? Are you there?"

I opened my mouth, but could only manage a croak. "Uh-huh."

"And that doesn't include the value of the gold, assuming we ever locate it."

"I found it," I said slowly. "That's what I wanted to tell you. It was out back. Buried under a tree. He told everyone he'd buried the goldfish." The gold now seemed like pocket change compared with the fortune my husband had amassed.

I glanced down at my shoes, the black leather Nine West platform loafers I'd bought on sale in the fall. Though he never hesitated to indulge his taste for fine clothes, I distinctly recall Roger yelling at me for buying those shoes, said I hadn't needed them. I remembered the time he made me return half the clothes I'd bought for Pete at Baby Gap; he said it was crazy to spend all that money on things he'd outgrow in six months. I remembered times we raced to get to Eggbert's before 8 A.M. to catch the early-bird special. The times we drove halfway across the country for vacation (with Pete crying miserably in his car seat) because it was cheaper than flying. I remembered how he painstakingly cut the twenty-five-cent coupon out of the Belgian waffle mix box, and how excited he was to discover we could get supermarket coupons online. On my 32nd birthday he bought me both volumes of the *Miser's Bible,* a book that shows you how to save money by recycling dryer lint and snotty tissues. Roger even suggested that I unravel

Pete's outgrown sweaters to reuse the yarn, but I didn't know how to knit.

"There's one outstanding bit of business," the investigator continued. "It's the condo on Lake Merle. I've got some information but I'd rather not discuss it until I'm absolutely sure."

"Is it good or bad?" I asked.

"I'd rather not say until I'm sure."

I admired her self-restraint, but her professionalism also irritated me. It had to be bad news. I could tell.

"I'll have a full report by Friday. Please hang in there until then, okay?"

I assured her I'd be fine. I heard the garage door open. It was Roger, home from his writers' retreat. He gamboled into the house, threw his overnight bag on the couch, and grabbed me. "Oh, how I've missed you," he whispered into my hair, moving a clammy hand under my sweatshirt.

"Roger, it's four o'clock. Pete's upstairs," I said.

"So? Let's tell him we need some cuddle time. We'll lock the door."

I'd have to be comatose to let Roger get on top of me. "I can't, honey." I almost choked on that last word. "I've got to take him for a haircut." A necessary lie and not too off the mark.

"Can't it wait?" He slipped a hand down my pants.

"No, it can't." I extracted his hand. I forced myself to kiss him.

"Maybe later." I detected a faint floral scent on his face.

'Til next time,

𝒱

February 6

I called Omar Sweet and told him what the investigator had uncovered. He let out a low whistle. His mind was already racing ahead. "Here's what we're going to do. Number one, keep playing dumb. Don't let him know you're onto him."

"I think I can manage that," I said.

"Next, we serve him with divorce papers."

I swallowed hard. Omar spoke so matter-of-factly about something I'd struggled with for so long. "And then what?"

"Then I take his deposition. Get him under oath, have him tally his net worth. What do you think he's likely to say?"

"I guess he'll say we've got a few hundred thousand. The house is worth about $250,000, we've got maybe $30,000 in savings, and another $20,000 in investments. That's it."

"Okay. Great. So he swears under oath that he's worth about $300,000. Then we show him the investigator's report. We take him to court. At this point we don't ask for half the assets. We ask the court to award *all* the assets and we've got a good chance of getting it because he will have lied under oath. Judges don't like that. Chances are the lawyer will quit because Roger lied to him as well, and lawyers don't like that. Your ex-husband will be in deep shit. And you'll be a very wealthy woman."

I told Omar that Libby had more news for me, and I was afraid it might be bad. He said we should wait until we have the full report before filing for divorce. I was disappointed. I had been so psyched up to finally serve him with papers. I didn't want to wait anymore, but I guess I had no choice.

'Til next time,

V

February 7

Took Pete to the pediatrician today. His hand is healing nicely, but there's probably going to be some scarring on his palm, enduring evidence of my negligence and irresponsibility.

Lynette Kohl-Chase stopped by with a tray of toffee brownies. "I thought you could use this," she said. I didn't let her past the screen door. I didn't want her to see my dirty kitchen floor, the McDonald's Happy Meal paraphernalia strewn across the family room, the plate of tangerine peels on the counter, the sticky trail of pancake syrup on the table.

I stared into her earnest face and asked, "Lynette, why do you persist in being so damned neighborly?"

She looked like she might cry and I felt like such a heel. "I'm sorry. I just thought, I mean, I can see you're going through a rough time. I thought you could use a little cheering up."

Now I was the one who wanted to cry. The woman was guileless. She had no idea that I viewed her existence as a reproach. "I'm sorry. You're just being nice and I'm being a bitch."

"No, you're not being a witch," she said, deftly sanitizing my remark. "You're just frazzled. I understand completely."

I wanted to say, How could you possibly understand? Instead, I took the tray and thanked her, then proceeded to devour half the brownies. Now I've got diarrhea, and I deserve that, too.

'Til next time,

V

February 8

I decided to distract myself by going to Borders and flipping through interior design magazines. Assuming I ever get Roger's money, I'm going to redo the kitchen. I bought a hot Chai and found a table in the back corner. This was a rare moment for me. I was alone, I had my Chai, and I was about to plunge into a stack of magazines. I couldn't wait to dig in. I was slipping off my jacket when I felt someone come up from behind and tug at my sleeves. "Let me help you with that."

It was Eddie. He put his mouth close to my ear and whispered, "How about joining me at the Holiday Inn?" His breath was like a hothouse, warm and moist. He was wearing soft black trousers, and a quick southerly glance confirmed that he was already excited. He noticed me noticing and smiled. Maybe it was the libido-squelching Prozac, or maybe it was my better judgment, but I knew I couldn't go with Eddie to the Holiday Inn. "Please. Eddie. You've got a wife. You have kids. It's just not right."

"That never stopped you before." He gripped my arm. "Don't tell me you're some kind of religious nut now. What, have you been *saved*?"

"No. It's nothing like that." I tried to pull my arm away. His fingers wrapped around my wrist in one of those martial arts grips that could break your bones if you tried to wriggle free.

"You're never going to get rid of me. You realize that, don't you?" He wasn't smiling. "You found it, didn't you?" he asked.

"Found what?" I answered, knowing precisely what he'd meant.

He reached out and turned my face toward his.

"Eddie, you're hurting me," I whispered.

"Look me right in the eyes and say it. Say, 'No, Eddie, I haven't found the gold.' "

"No, Eddie, I haven't found the gold." I repeated. "Now please take your hands off me."

"You're lying." He stared at me. I was scared. This felt like such a violation, of my body and space and head. I wanted only to spend twenty minutes in Borders drinking hot Chai and reading interior design magazines. I grabbed my jacket and walked out. With everything going on in my life now, the last thing I need to worry about is a volatile ex-lover.

'Til next time,
V

February 9

I can't bring myself to visit my parents today. I know I should spend time with my father while I still have him. But it's so demoralizing to see Dad so small, so old, so ill. Am I being selfish by staying away? Or am I being self-protective?

'Til next time,
V

February 10

The phone rang at 9:07. It was Libby. "I've got to tell you, Ms. Ryan, I've investigated a number of interesting and rather provocative cases, but nothing quite like this."

"Please, Libby, just say what you have to say."

"Okay." She sucked in her breath. "I confirmed that Mr. Tisdale does indeed own the condo on Lake Merle."

"And . . . ?"

"And it's not an investment property."

"Let me guess. That's where he keeps his other wife, right?" I joked.

But Libby wasn't laughing.

"Libby. Say something." I closed my eyes and prayed. God, if you have even an ounce of compassion left for me, please don't let Roger have another wife. I held my breath.

"Her name is Mary," the investigator began. "Tisdale, obviously."

Why is that obvious? I wanted to say. I remembered how Roger and I had fought when I told him I wanted to keep my maiden name. He called me a "feminazi," said I should be happy to give up my family name. He insisted that Ryan was ordinary, working-class, "like a can of Spam." Evidently Roger managed to find a woman who willingly fulfilled his macho compulsion to brand his wife with his lousy name.

"Listen," Libby said softly, "maybe we should have the rest of this conversation in person."

"No, Libby," I pleaded. "Now. Please. Tell me the rest."

"It looks as if they've been married since June. Married in the Sullivan County courthouse, by a justice of the peace. Judge Olcott Hanes."

"Children?" I asked weakly. I crossed my fingers and prayed again.

"We don't know yet," Libby responded. "Listen. Are you okay?"

"What the hell do you think?" I snapped. Another wife? My head was spinning.

I needed time, time to sort things out. Just when I thought I knew the depths of Roger's depravity, just when I felt that God had given me all I could handle, I find out that my husband has *another wife!* Who was she? Where had he met her? How did he find time to be with her? How could he have cheated on not one but *two* wives when he was screwing around with Alyssa and God knows who else? Was she young? Was she pretty? Was she a good cook? And most important, was she entitled to any of his assets?

"I'm sorry I was short with you," I told Libby. "That was uncalled for."

"No problem," she answered. "I'm accustomed to it. Comes with the territory. I tend to be the purveyor of bad news. It's not like people hire me to find out what their husbands are buying them for Valentine's Day."

"When do you think you'll know more?" I asked. My head felt like it was going to explode. I grabbed the Advil off the lazy Susan in the kitchen cabinet and swallowed four. Libby said she would call me as soon as she uncovered anything else.

Omar insists it's unlikely that Mary Tisdale is entitled to any of Roger's assets since I married him first. That was the most reassuring thing I'd heard all day, assuming it's true. Omar reminded me to keep up a good front. I don't know how much longer I can fake this. I want that man out of my house. I wish he were dead.

'Til next time,

V

February 11

It's 1 P.M. and I still haven't heard from Libby. This is agonizing! I left messages with her answering service, but she hasn't called back. I had expected to go with Roger to visit his parents. I begged off, told him I was having menstrual cramps. That's the one excuse that always placates him; he never argues with gynecological alibis. I'm still reeling. I can't wait for Libby to call back.

'Til next time,

V

February 12

I'm trying to stay focused but I can barely breathe. I know Roger is depraved, and believe me, I know I'm

better off without him, but I still can't help feeling
like a loser and a reject. I wasn't wife enough for him,
so he had to find himself another one? And this one
is undoubtedly the prim and proper traditionalist he
has always wanted: the cook, the housekeeper, the
submissive little woman who gladly dispenses with
her family name to take on the Tisdale moniker. Who
was this woman? Where had he found her? And how,
in a town this size, could he possibly get away with
it?

Pete's play date with Patrick Green fell through,
which meant I had to serve as entertainment director. Pete must have sensed something was seriously
wrong because he wouldn't leave me alone all day.
We played cards and forty-six rounds of Candy
Land, watched Barney videos (gag) and made two
and a half pounds of pink spaghetti with the Play-
Doh Fun Factory. Then he insisted on singing from
a big songbook my mother had bought him for
Christmas. All the songs are long and repetitive, the
kind of music that kids sing on long car drives when
they want to make their parents crazy. We were
singing "There's a Hole in the Bucket," and when
we got to the line where the wife tells her husband
to fix the hole with a straw, Pete asked, "How can
straw fix a hole in a bucket, Mommy?" And before I
could stop myself, I shrieked, "It can't, Petey, which
is why this song sucks!" He just stared at me. I

laughed and tried to make a little joke of it, but I think I scared him.

'Til next time,

V

February 13

Roger came home unexpectedly from play rehearsal today. He didn't realize I was in the downstairs bathroom, and when I collided with him, he seemed nervous. He had a mesh bag of daffodil bulbs in one hand, a spade in the other. He claimed he wanted to do some planting. Roger has always hated gardening. In fact, his exact words were, "I hate nature." And nobody plants daffodils this time of year.

"What a great idea!" I exclaimed. "Let me grab my bulb-digger thingy. I'd love to help."

He stuck out a hand to stop me. "That's quite all right. I'd like to do it myself. I mean, I'm sure you have better things to do."

"Don't be silly," I said. "I'm totally free. Remember, I'm unemployed."

Roger managed a shaky laugh. "Why don't you relax? Take a bath!"

I relented. "Actually, I could use a hot soak right now. Pulled a muscle carrying groceries."

"Okay, then." Roger wiped the perspiration from his forehead. I sprinted upstairs to the bathroom, locked the door, and ran the water for effect. I carefully opened the blinds in the bathroom. I saw Roger begin digging under the blue spruce. I watched him plunge the spade into the earth, deeper and deeper and deeper. He wiped his brow, then plunged again. He dropped to the ground and put his hands into the soil. He grabbed the shovel and started digging again. A second hole. Then a third. And yet another. Forty minutes later the yard looked like a habitat for prairie dogs. It reminded me of a book Pete has, a story about a poor lad who gets duped by a leprechaun. The story ends with this guy digging under every tree in the forest. Naturally, he never finds the gold. And neither did Roger.

Later, as he was brushing his teeth, he asked, "Did you happen to find anything that, er, belongs to me?"

I tried not to smile. "Like what?"

"Oh, a little box, like a strongbox. I kept some files in there. You know, for my next play."

"No, sweetheart, I haven't seen it. But I'll let you know if I do."

'Til next time,

V

February 15

Libby finally called. She had no information about Mary Tisdale. She doesn't know how they met, whether they have kids, how old she is, where she's from. No one in the Lake Merle condos would say whether they had met her, or whether she even exists. There are no official records for Mary Tisdale, no social security number, no driver's license, no insurance records. Libby drove out to the condo twice and banged on the door, but no one answered. All the shades were drawn, the lights were off. "But I'm sure there was someone inside," she said. "I could hear music. And I smelled something cooking."

"So what's the next step?" I asked. "Can we involve the police? Get a warrant or something?"

Libby thought for a moment. "I'll call you right back." Ten minutes later, Libby was on the line. "I've got a friend in the sheriff's department. She says she thinks she can wrangle a warrant next week. Maybe Wednesday. Can you wait that long?"

"I guess I'll have to." I felt deflated. But when I hung up, I decided that no, I couldn't wait that long. This weekend I'm going to drive out to Lake Merle myself, and I'm not leaving until I've met Mrs. Mary Tisdale.

'Til next time,

V

February 16

I never made it to Lake Merle. It was around noon when the phone rang. Roger had taken Pete to the mall for shoes. I was home alone.

"Open your front door," Eddie told me.

"Why should I?" I answered. I wasn't in the mood for his games.

"Just do it."

I was on the cordless phone. "Fine," I told him. "I'm walking downstairs. I'm opening the door . . ."

There he was, parked in the driveway, talking to me from his cell phone. He slid down the window and blew me a kiss. He kept talking into the phone, staring at me. "Wanna go for a ride?"

I went back in the house and locked the door behind me. "Not now, Eddie. Please."

He sighed long and hard. "Don't be this way, darling," he said.

"Do you realize I could take a restraining order out on you?"

Silence. Then he finally said, "Oh, you don't want to do that, sweetheart. I'm not your enemy. Besides, don't you want me on your side when you take your husband to court? Especially when you guys start fighting about custody. Don't you want me on your side?"

This was a nightmare. "Look. What do you want from me? Money? Sex?"

Eddie chortled. "How about a little of both? Come on out. Let's take a ride."

I grabbed my purse and climbed into his van. He leaned over and kissed me and his mouth was hot and sweet. The slick seats smelled of Armorall. He drove out to the abandoned grain silo by the county airport. And then, amidst the pesticides and peat moss in his van, Eddie kissed my neck and whispered, "I missed you." He started fiddling with my belt buckle.

"Eddie, please. I have to get back home."

"Not yet, darling," he whispered. He reached under my shirt and casually played with my breasts as he spoke. "We're not done . . . negotiating."

"What do you want, Eddie? Gold? Is that what this is all about?"

A smile slowly spread across his face. "You're a genius."

"I don't have the gold," I told him. He pinched my nipple. "Ouch!" I yelled. "Let go!" I pulled away. "Eddie, I'm perfectly happy to give you a little cash if you're short. Just tell me what you need."

He laughed. " 'A little cash' isn't exactly what I had in mind."

"Eddie, there is no gold. Diana was wrong."

Eddie stared into my face. He didn't know whether to believe me.

Finally, he said, "Really?"

I nodded solemnly. "Really."

"In that case, I guess I'll take you home now." He turned the key in the ignition and I gulped back a lump in my throat. Neither of us spoke during the ride back. He switched on a country station and hummed quietly. I wondered whether there was any way Eddie might discover I had lied to him. When he pulled into my neighborhood, I reached for the door. "You can let me out right here." I jumped out and walked the quarter of a mile to my house.

It is now 3 P.M. Roger and Pete should be back any minute. My nipple still hurts.

'Til next time,
V

February 17

2:45 A.M. I'm sitting here, waiting for the Tylenol PM to take effect. I can't sleep. I can't get the image out of my head of Eddie heaving over my body in the van. I swear I can still smell him on me. I'm completely obsessed with the following horrible thoughts: (1) Eddie will realize that I'm lying and he'll try to hurt me. (2) Eddie will realize I'm lying and he'll kill Pete. (3) Eddie has given me AIDS. (4) Eddie has given me herpes. (5) Eddie has given me genital warts. (6) I'm pregnant.

I'm finally feeling a little sleepy. I think I'm going to crash on the couch now. I can't lie next to Roger, for all the obvious reasons—and now this. I feel sick. But tired too, thank God. I've got to get at least a few hours' sleep if I'm going to drive out to Lake Merle tomorrow.

'Til next time,
V

February 18

I never thought I'd make it out of the house. First Pete said that he was still hungry after lunch, so I made him a cup of tomato soup and a peanut butter sandwich. He then announced that he hated crunchy peanut butter. We were all out of creamy. So I trashed the sandwich and made him tortellini instead. The colander tipped as I was draining the pasta, and the whole thing slid down the garbage disposal. Pete started screaming and flailing his arms and legs. He kicked off a shoe, which hit the mirror in the hall, shattering it into a million jagged pieces. I grabbed for the glass with my bare hands, cut my index finger, and bled on the carpet. I couldn't find the carpet cleaner and tried dishwashing liquid, which only made it worse.

When I finally settled Pete down, Roger appeared and announced that he wanted to make summer plans. He thought it might be nice if Pete and I spent the summer in the Upper Peninsula, and maybe he could visit us on weekends. I played along, told him it was a splendid idea. That creep had it all figured out. He'd spend Monday through Friday on Lake Merle with his other wife, spend weekends with me, *and never the twain shall meet*. That's what he thinks!

After Roger had plotted out our summer using his

new calendar software, the phone rang. And rang. And rang. First it was Greta Haas from church, asking if I'd help with this year's Easter egg hunt. Then my mother called, just to complain about Dad's oncologist; she says he ran down the hospital fire escape just to avoid talking to her, and I believe it. Then a supposedly wheelchair-bound phone solicitor with Handicapped Marketing Associates tried to sell me light bulbs that supposedly last 100 years. (I pushed the button on my new anti-telemarketer gadget—it gives me such pleasure to use that thing—and listened delightedly as the authoritative recorded voice told the phone solicitor to shove it.) The phone rang one more time, but whoever was on the line hung up. Caller ID registered this one as an anonymous call. My guess is, it was the phone solicitor calling me back for spite. Or maybe it was Eddie.

By now it was 3 P.M. I told Roger I had to get my nails done. He nodded vaguely in my direction and returned his attention to *Xena*. I'm sure it didn't even register that I'd left the house. Twenty minutes later he would call upstairs for me, starting with a medium-range holler, gradually building up to that shrill eardrum-puncturing shriek of his. He would ask Pete to run upstairs and find me, at which point Pete would tell him that I left to get my nails done because Pete, unlike his father, actually paid attention when I had something to say. I imagined the stupid way Roger rubbed the side of his head whenever he was bewildered, and thanked God I wouldn't have to live with this dog much longer.

I took the shortcut to Lake Merle, but hit a detour—they're digging up Crawford Road—which meant I had to take Market, putting me twenty minutes out of my way. By the time I'd made it to the lake I had soaked through my blazer and my hands were so sweaty I left stains on the leather-wrapped steering wheel. I pulled into the subdivision, followed the road west, and found Roger's condo. It was the last unit at the very end of a gravel road virtually engulfed by tall pines. I parked along the curb. My heart thumped so hard I could see the silver teapot pin on my lapel pulsating.

I stared at the condo. While most of the units had some special feature—a striped awning here, a hand-painted mailbox there—this one had nothing to distinguish it. The landscaping was sparse, almost barren. There were no painted shutters, no pretty plaque bearing the family name or house number, no colorful wind sock. In fact, there were no signs of life. The shades and curtains were all drawn. Visitors, it seems, were not welcome here.

I turned my ear toward the door and listened. Backstreet Boys. I heard a faint rustling, footsteps, something clanging, maybe a pan. I took another deep breath and knocked at the door, softly at first, then harder when no one responded. I knocked again. The music stopped, and then I could hear nothing. No footsteps, no clanging. I cupped my ear against the door now, and held my breath until it hurt.

The door opened. I lifted my eyes and saw the apprehensive face of a young girl, a small and slender Asian girl. She opened the door a crack and stared at me. She couldn't have been older than sixteen. She wore a plain white buttoned shirt and cheap, shiny trousers, white socks, and flip-flops. And she was beautiful. Full lips, dark eyes. Her black hair was tied back. No makeup except for lip gloss. She was chewing gum.

"Is the lady of the house here?" I asked her. She stared at me as if she didn't understand.

I tried again. "Do you speak English?" She nodded quickly, but kept her grip on the door.

"The lady of the house. Mary Tisdale. Is she home?"

She looked at me a long time. "I am Mrs. Tisdale."

I thought I must have heard wrong. What do you mean, you're Mary Tisdale? Crazy thoughts popped into my head. Maybe she was a distant cousin, from the Asian side of the family (but there is no Asian side of the family). Maybe a half sister—my father-in-law's illegitimate daughter. I groped for a rational explanation. How could this be Roger's wife?

Impossible. I tried to remain composed, but my heart was now smashing around in my mouth, and I could feel my whole body flush with panic.

"What's your husband's name?"

She beamed at me. "Roger Tisdale. Mister Roger Tisdale." Jesus. She was a kid. I felt dizzy, heard my blood roaring in my ears. I steadied myself against the door frame.

"Let me get this straight. You are married—you're married, as in husband and wife—to Roger Tisdale?"

She nodded her head enthusiastically.

"Roger Tisdale, the playwright?"

"Yes! Yes! That's my man!" the girl exclaimed. Her man? I had to stay clearheaded. I had to keep her talking. I suddenly regretted that I didn't have any M&M's with me; she struck me as the kind of kid who could be bribed with candy.

"What's your business?" she asked, a little suspiciously.

"My business? Oh, I live around here; just wanted to meet the neighbors and all that. I'm Mrs. Ryan."

Mary started to smile, then remembered something and grew serious. She closed the door a little more. "I'm not supposed to talk to anybody."

"Why not?"

"My husband says not to. He says, 'Stay inside and take good care, Mary.' So that's what I do. I stay inside and wait for him." She pouted. "But I miss him. He's all the time traveling, putting on his shows."

Putting on his shows? So that's how he explained why he's rarely around. With me it was writers' retreats and rehearsals. With her, he's putting on shows. Dandy.

A pregnant cat rubbed against her legs. She lifted it into her arms and stroked its head. "I play with Tippy. Eat. Watch TV. Dance to music. Clean house. That's all I do."

I tried to be solicitous, tried to be a nice, normal, nonthreatening woman. A friend. A big sister. "Oh, I know what you mean. Sounds like my life." I rolled my eyes.

"Men."

She smiled at me and echoed: "Men."

"Listen, can I come in for a minute? I'm feeling a little sick. I think . . . I may be pregnant." I don't know, it just seemed like the right thing to say. I could almost hear her interior debate: Roger told me not to talk to strangers. But this lady seems nice. Maybe it's okay. And Roger won't find out anyway.

I prayed hard while she considered my request. Please make her let me in. Please, Lord. Finally, she stepped back and pulled open the door. "I guess it's okay," she said.

I recognized the furniture right away. The place was filled with the crap we'd kept in the basement for the garage sale we never had the energy to have. Roger had loaded everything into the back of a U-Haul. He said he'd deliver it to Promise House, the

battered women's shelter. I spotted the pair of but-
terfly chairs, the cheap laminate bookcases, the
wicker love seat and chairs we bought in graduate
school at Pier 1. Hanging above the sofa, the ama-
teurish still life I'd painted when I was nine months
pregnant and bored out of my skull. I'm not sure
what galled me more, that he gave her something I
painted or that he gave her something so hideous.
What I did not see, however, was a telephone. Leave
it to Roger to lock this girl in the condo without a
connection to the outside world. "Can I use your
phone?" I asked.

"Oh, we can't have phones out here in the country," she said matter-of-factly. "And my husband says
the kind without wires are too expensive. Is that the
kind you have? Without wires?"

"Yes, that's what we have. The kind without
wires." God.

I watched her size five bottom as she led me to the
sofa, and I cringed imagining Roger violating her
body. She made Alyssa look matronly. I couldn't pin-
point the accent. Filipino, maybe? She offered me a
glass of water. I reached to accept it and gestured for
her to sit down. She sat cross-legged in the wicker
chair and the cat jumped into her lap, kneaded her
little belly, and plopped down. I glanced around the
room. It was sparsely furnished but spotless, truly
immaculate. I had a cruel, fleeting thought—maybe
she could clean our other house too. I attribute this

bizarre thought to my state: completely deranged. My husband had a child for a wife. He kept her locked in a little condo at the end of a country road with instructions to stay put. For the moment, I had two goals: to learn her age, and to figure out how they met.

Mary broke the silence. "When's the baby coming?"

I didn't know what she meant until I remembered my lie. "Oh, I'm not sure. Maybe in the winter." I was speaking like a foreigner myself. I was trying to establish some kind of rapport.

She rolled the cat over and displayed its bulging belly. "Tippy's pregnant too!" She ran her fingers over the nipples. She smiled and patted her own stomach. "I also want to have baby."

"Are you"—I tried to produce a smile—"pregnant?"

The girl shrugged. "Don't know. Maybe." She pulled the gum out of her mouth, stretched it, and popped it back in. She smiled dreamily. "Maybe not. Hope so. I love babies."

Of course you do, I wanted to say, because you're practically a zygote yourself. "Babies are great," I answered. "Do you have any little brothers or sisters?"

She looked away. "Yes. Four brothers, three sisters. Back home."

Now I was getting somewhere. "Oh, what a nice big family. Are you the oldest?"

The girl nodded, still looking away. "How old are you?" I asked, then held my breath.

She bit her lip and hesitated. "Twenty-one."

Bullshit. I giggled and said, "No, really. How old are you, really?"

She looked at me and answered almost obediently. "Sixteen, ma'am."

Now I was ma'am? I should have been glad to get my answer, but now I was stewing because she called me ma'am. There was that wretched word again. "You're a beautiful girl, Mary," I told her. "You must be an actress. Is that how you met your husband?"

I'd flattered her. She smiled shyly. "Oh, no. Not me. I met him through CLIT."

"*Excuse* me?"

"You know, Classy Ladies International Trade." When she realized I hadn't heard of this CLIT, she elaborated: "It's a worldwide organization that links well-mannered international ladies with established American gentlemen." She obviously had that memorized. I wondered if she knew what the acronym meant in English. I would have laughed if I hadn't been so mortified.

"How nice," I answered. I didn't know what to say next. Should I tell her I was Roger's real wife? Let her know her marriage is a joke, that she's essentially a sex slave? I didn't want to say anything that might scare her, and I couldn't let Roger know I was onto him. Not yet, not until Omar gave me the go-ahead.

So I pulled myself up, thanked her for the water, and started to leave. But I felt such compassion for the girl. She was stuck in that little condo with all my old crap. No car, no friends. I had to ask, "Listen, do you need anything?"

"Oh, no. We're fine. We have everything we need," she said, trying to sound like a grown-up.

I sped home, avoiding the detour this time, and called Omar, then Libby. Then I got online and searched for Classy Ladies International Trade. And I cannot believe what I discovered. Much more, later.

'Til next time,

V

February 19

I was anxious to tell Omar the news about Roger's mail-order bride. He reacted with uncharacteristic zeal. "Woo-hoo!" he yelped. "We're going to nail that bastard to the wall!" I loved hearing him talk tough, and his enthusiasm filled me with pure joy. (I know this is an issue for me, and I realize it's not particularly healthy—my impulse to make Omar my hero, my knight, my personal Terminator. Rather than see him merely as my well-paid advocate, I've already romanticized our relationship and his role in my life. I love his bald, penile head.) Omar said we're ready to serve Roger with the divorce papers. I told him I wanted to wait until Friday. I've decided that I want to be there when he opens the envelope. I need just a little more time. Jesus. It's really happening.

I suspect Libby was a bit rankled to hear that I drove out to Lake Merle myself and got to Mary before she did. Libby didn't say anything at first, and for a second I thought we'd been disconnected. To her credit, she recovered gracefully. "Hey, you want a job?" she joked. "I could always use the help."

Even though I'm glad I took the initiative, I'm annoyed she didn't do it first. She's the investigator. I'm just an unemployed psychotherapist. What's the point of paying her all this money if I'm doing the legwork?

Libby said she's going to go out to the condo and get some pictures of Mary for her report. She also said she'd try to contact Classy Ladies International Trade, but suspects they'll be slow to produce records if they suspect they're part of an investigation and if the girl is underage.

I went on-line, typed in classyladiesinternational trade.com. Lo and behold, it was there, in all its putridity. The on-line "catalog" was filled with 145 thumbnail shots of women of all ages, shapes, and sizes. Most of them were surprisingly plain, and many looked sad, though they obviously tried their best to look "marketable" for the camera. I was particularly struck by "Jasmine," a plump woman who claimed to be thirty-five but who looked closer to fifty. When I clicked on her thumbnail, I got the full dossier. She said she loved housecleaning and cooking, and promised to make a cozy home for her Western mate. She looked panic-stricken.

The company is owned by H. Wilhem Prost, a character who brazenly describes himself the "proud owner" of a Filipina bride. He sprinkles his own sickening experiences throughout the site. An excerpt from the home page:

Willing, compliant, obedient. Let our ladies take you back in time, a time when men wore the pants and women did as they were told. Imagine your own geisha girl at your beck and call, a girl who only has eyes for you. Gentlemen, these women are desperate to meet upstanding Western men like yourselves. And all our ladies come with a 100 percent money-back guarantee. If you are not absolutely satisfied with your CLIT girl, you can return her—postage paid—and choose another of our lovely girls. What's your fantasy? Damsel in distress? Virgin bride? Betty Crocker? Barefoot and pregnant? Young and innocent? We've got them all, and plenty more. CLIT girls won't tell you it's your turn to do the dishes or cook dinner. They wouldn't dream of getting a job (unless, of course, you tell them to). Their greatest pleasure is to serve, whether in the kitchen or in the

bedroom. These are women who truly appreciate Western men, who crave the comfort of a
traditional, domestic life. All they want in this
world is a Western man who will treat them like
a lady. If you're that kind of man—and who
isn't?—then we have the girl for you!

I thought of Mary, sitting alone in the condo beneath my ugly painting, playing with the cat, chewing gum. I wonder if that's what she had in mind
when she left her homeland and family. I tried not to
imagine the fantasies Mary was purchased to fulfill.
In graduate school, I once heard Roger tell his buddy
Kirby Bond that "there's nothing in this world like a
cherry," and I actually thought they were talking
about produce until I saw his wicked grin and realized, blushing, that he was talking about something
else entirely.

'Til next time,

V

February 21

I felt masochistically compelled to go to the CLIT
Web site again today. A disgusting sample of the
FAQs:

Q: How much will it cost me to get a CLIT girl?
A: $6,450 total, American dollars. (A drop in

the bucket compared with what it costs to maintain and eventually get rid of the typical American wife.)

Q: Will my bride speak English?
A: Enough to understand and fulfill your every wish. Seriously, most Filipinas speak English. They also speak other native languages, like Tagalog, Ilocano, and Visayan. If your bride needs help learning your mother tongue, you can surely play Professor Higgins to her Eliza Doolittle—we guarantee that she will be a willing student!

Q: How young are your girls?
A: Officially speaking, we can't get girls younger than sixteen, because the government won't give them a visa. But some clever girls will fudge their records, and we're certainly not tattling on them!! (Wink!) If you have a hankering for youth, let us know, and we'll see what we can do.

Q: Can I do anything I want to my Filipina bride?
A: As long as she consents, of course! But we don't abide abuse or misuse of any kind, so if you're planning on beating your bride or worse, don't expect our support when your sorry ass gets hauled into court!

Q: Would a girl in her teens or twenties be interested in a gentleman in his forties or fifties?
A: Absolutely! Filipinas respect and admire older men. As the proud owner of my own Filipina bride (my fourth and last wife, I assure you), I can tell you that they admire experience and maturity. And if it takes us older gents a little longer in matters romantic, all the better for them.

Q: Aren't mail-order brides for American geeks who can't get lucky with their own kind?
A: We get this question all the time—from spoiled American women. The short answer: No. International brides are for discerning gentlemen who are simply sick and tired of playing games with jaded, grasping, greedy, selfish American women. And who isn't? You only live once, gentlemen. Why not live well? CLIT can make it happen for you. Call us now!

Unbelievable! As I scanned the site I imagined what must have been going through my husband's debauched brain when he decided he just had to have one of these poor girls. Either he has some kind of tumor pressing on whatever part of the brain regulates morality or he has succumbed to another condition—the complete eradication of reason and conscience that apparently accompanies wealth in some people. I had a client like that, the wife of an Internet mogul. She regularly abused the illegal aliens she hired as housekeepers. Convinced a maid had stolen some jewelry, she pulled on a Playtex glove and conducted her own cavity search. She found nothing, and fired her anyway.

Living with Roger this week has been absolute torture. I feel like the kid in *Sixth Sense*. I'm the only one who knows he's dead. This sucker has no idea that the demolition ball's about to smash him right in the face. I pray nothing goes wrong. Omar keeps saying it's like the Battle of Normandy. We don't make a move until we're completely ready.

By tomorrow morning, Libby's report will be in my hands, with a copy on Omar's desk. Friday at noon, it's *boom, baby*. I can hardly wait to see the look on his face when the sheriff's deputy serves him with the divorce papers. I cannot wait!

'Til next time,

𝒱

February 28

Today at 4 P.M. my parents came home from the oncologist to discover that the front door had been jimmied open, and the house was torn apart. At first it seemed like nothing valuable was missing. Not my mother's jewelry, or the silverware, or the cash in Dad's sock drawer.

When my father saw the mess, he collapsed and chipped his front teeth when he hit the tiled floor. My mother called 911, screaming incoherently. The dispatcher sent a police car and an ambulance.

Mom had revived my father by the time the paramedics arrived, and sent them away. The police searched the house, found nothing substantive, then called me. I sped through every red light on the way to my parents' house. When I got there, the police were already gone, Dad was asleep, and Mom was making a pot of peppermint-ginseng tea. A locksmith was busy at the side door, replacing the cheap old lock with a more secure deadbolt.

"The police think it's neighborhood kids," my mother told me as she pulled a pair of mugs out of the cabinet. Her eyes were swollen from crying. "Said they were probably looking for drugs—painkillers. That happens sometimes, you know. When kids get wind of someone dying."

The word hung there. Until then, neither of us had ever admitted that Dad was dying. Until then, we spoke only of temporary setbacks.

"Shhh!" I scolded. "What if he hears you?"

My mother smiled sadly. "I wouldn't worry about that, love." The air was sour with the smell of incontinence and decay. Engulfed by the demands of caregiving, my mother had stopped tending herself; her fingernails were broken and there was a swath of dull gray across her otherwise red hair. As painful as it was to see my father so diminished, it was agonizing to see this change in my mother—a woman who wouldn't dream of being seen without makeup, not even for the moment it takes to run out to the curb and retrieve the mail. I watched her at the sink, her thickened waistline and slumped shoulders, and forced myself to think of something else.

Mom had just put the cozy over the teapot when the phone rang. I told her to let the machine pick up, but she insisted on answering, thinking it might be the police, or maybe Dad's doctor. I heard her say, "Excuse me?" then turned to see a look of confusion on her face. Then she said, "Who *is* this?" and I just knew this had something to do with me.

"What was that all about, Mom?"

"I don't know. Weird," she said. She poured the tea into my mug. "It was a man."

My heart thudded. "What did he say, Mom? Tell me."

My mother looked at me. "He said, 'Tell your daughter I found what I was looking for.' " She took a sip. "Weird, huh?"

I raced upstairs to the crawlspace, slid open the door, and frantically reached inside. The strongbox. It was gone. The gold was gone. I started crying, screaming, tearing at my hair, my clothes. I felt sick, rootless, panicked, despairing, desperate. Not because the gold was gone, but because the man who had been my lover had forced his way into a dying man's house and ripped it apart with those big, callused hands. I told my mother about my suspicions and she looked at me with scorn. She folded her arms across her chest and whispered, "What have you gotten yourself into, Valerie?" I felt like a child, chastised and shamed.

My mother urged me to call the police, but what would I tell them? That my former lover had stolen the gold ingots I'd stolen from my soon-to-be exhusband? I told Mom not to worry, that I'd handle everything. I helped her clean up the mess, then tucked her into bed beside my father, and locked up behind me. I went to the Jeep, locked all the doors, and sat there in my parents' driveway.

'Til next time,

V

March 1

When I woke up this morning, I realized that my marriage would be over in less than twenty-four hours. I should have been exultant, but I felt like I was crawling out of my skin. Hoping to distract myself, I headed to the gym for a sweaty, mindless workout. I grabbed a battered *People* and found an empty treadmill. Nine minutes and fourteen burnt calories later, Ben Murphy clambered onto the machine next to mine and gave me one of his unselfconsciously openhearted smiles. "You're looking healthy," he said. In my family, "healthy" was a euphemism for fat, but I believe that Ben believed that I looked healthy.

Ben Murphy reminds me of my neighbor Anne's golden retriever. He always seems so darn happy to see me. He told me that this summer he and his son will take a cross-country trip to visit historical battlefields. Personally, I can't think of a worse way to spend my vacation, but I didn't have the heart to tell him that.

"It's going to be quite the adventure," he said, sprinting effortlessly at 5.9 miles an hour (I was only walking 3.5 mph and was already panting). "We're going south to the Moores Creek National Battlefield in North Carolina, and probably hit the Wright Brothers National Memorial while we're down there. Then there's the Cowpens National Battlefield in South Carolina—that's where the British advanced on the Pickens militia." His voice rose with excitement. I tried to look interested. I had no idea what he was talking about. The only thing I remember about social studies is Harriet Tubman: Runaway Slave. I bought a book about her from the Scholastic Book Club. I remember its smooth brick red cover, the smell of its fresh pages, the story of brave Harriet. Everything else is a blur. Even now, when I watch C-SPAN, I'm more likely to take note of a senator's blubbery chin than anything he has to say about tax reform.

". . . but I think the Antietam Battlefield in Sharpsville, Maryland, will be the most dramatic." Ben was still talking. "That historical site marks the end of Robert E. Lee's first invasion of the North. Over twenty-three thousand troops were killed or wounded in a single day." Ben shook his head. "Can you believe that? Twenty-three thousand men in one day. Boggles the mind."

"Yes, it does," I answered. What really boggled my mind is that someone so different from me—a keen, unaffected, earnest, American-history-loving chemistry professor—seemed to be interested in me. I wondered whether I could return the attraction, whether I could find long-term happiness with someone who reads the *Journal of Quantitative Spectroscopy and Radiative Transfer*. Maybe he's exactly what I need right now. I wonder what he's like in bed. Based on the way he kissed me that day in the car, I'm willing to bet he's not half bad.

'Til next time,

V

March 2

I had a new plan. I would take Mary home with me and together we would confront Roger.

I drove out to Lake Merle, pulled up to 144 Lark's Way, and jumped out of the car. I braced myself for Tippy, the pregnant cat. But Tippy never appeared, and neither, it turned out, did Mary. The blinds were all drawn, just as they were last time, but now I knew there was no life behind those windows. I pressed my ear to the door, but heard no music, no clanging of pans. I rapped softly, then a bit harder, then kicked, but there was no answer. I went to the back and pried at a window. It slid open.

The place was empty. The wicker furniture, my ugly painting, the bookcases—nothing remained! I called out the girl's name and listened for her light footsteps, but there were none.

How could she have disappeared? Where had she gone? All at once I had the most overpowering urge to run back to the Jeep, the same feeling I'd had as a kid running up the stairs from the basement, suddenly petrified for no good reason.

I called Libby from my cell phone. A computerized voice reported that the number was no longer in service. I was anxious to share the news with someone. I tried Omar but his secretary said he'd be out of the office all day. I called my best friend Betsy, but her phone just rang and rang. I drove past Ben Murphy on the way home and waved at him but he looked right through me, as if he didn't even know me. I'd never felt so utterly alone.

I looked at my watch. It was noon. Omar said the

divorce papers would be served between 1:00 and 2:00. I had to get home in time. Every nerve ending in my body buzzed. My tongue and fingers and feet felt like they were shooting sparks.

When I got into the house, I could hear Roger in the shower, singing happily. I arranged myself casually in the family room, snapped on the TV, then snapped it off. Couldn't bear the noise, the lights, the color. My head felt like it was filling with helium. I thought I would either float away or explode. Eventually, the sound of water flowing through pipes ceased, and Roger was padding across the upstairs hall in his slippers. He called down, "Home already, love?"

"Yes, honey," I called back. My voice cracked, and "honey" came out like some awful croaking noise, like a frog flattened under the wheel of a semi. I glanced nervously toward the window. Omar had said that a sheriff's deputy would be delivering the papers, but the car that arrived at precisely 1 P.M. was an ordinary Ford Taurus, and the man who got out was wearing an Abercrombie and Fitch T-shirt and jeans. I figured that the sheriff's deputy had more important things to do than serve divorce papers to philandering husbands, and this guy was just filling in.

The man checked the envelope, then the address on our mailbox. I decided to go out to the back deck so Roger would have to be the one to open the door.

I heard the knock, then Roger's footsteps tripping down the stairs. I heard, "Roger Tisdale?" And then something I couldn't make out.

I reappeared and watched as my husband stared at the envelope.

"What could this be?" he mused aloud.

"I don't know," I told him. "Why don't you go ahead and open it?"

"Fabulous idea." He offered me a toothy grin and pulled out the papers. He examined them, but said nothing.

"Well, aren't you going to say something?" I asked. I had the uneasy feeling that something had gone wrong. Roger just smiled at me.

"You're a piece of work, you know that?" He handed me the paper. "I believe this is meant for you, my sweet."

I snatched the paper from Roger's hand. At first glance I could see it was a picture, a photograph, actually a Xerox of a photo with a line of type underneath, a caption. I thought it was a newspaper clipping, and in my disoriented state I thought it was some kind of divorce announcement, a newspaper wedding announcement in reverse.

Then I realized it was a picture of me and Eddie in bed at the Econolodge. I read the caption again and again, unable to make sense of it, unwilling to believe it.

It said, simply, "You lose."

I felt a boiling wave roll up my body, an enveloping sense of disorientation. This couldn't be happening. My husband grinned like a hyena. I stared at the picture until my eyes burned from the fumes of the ink on the page. Only one person could have snapped that picture, and I vowed that if I ever got my hands on her, I'd rip her lungs out.

"What, exactly, were you expecting, my precious?" Roger squinted at me. "Let's see. . . . Could it have been . . . divorce papers, perhaps?" He snapped his head back and roared with laughter. "Oh! I wish you could see the look on your face. Priceless!" He wiped tears from his eyes and pointed at me. "Priceless!"

I grabbed the phone and punched in Libby's number. Roger sneered, "Let me guess. You're calling your private investigator, right?" How could he have known that? I slammed down the phone and raced out to the Jeep, locked all the doors, and picked up my cell phone. I could see Roger watching me from the doorway, laughing harder than ever.

After a few shrill rings, I got that same recording again. I tried Omar next, but the secretary wouldn't put me through. When I gave her my name and insisted on speaking to him immediately, she said he wasn't taking on any more new clients. I frantically explained that I wasn't new, that I'd already retained him. She insisted that she didn't have my name in the files! "That's impossible," I cried, the knot in my stomach now wedged in my throat. "Look under Ryan. R-Y-A-N. Or maybe Tisdale, my husband's name. T-I-S-D-A-L-E."

The secretary sighed. "Okay. I'll check again."

I bit the insides of my cheeks and waited. Dear God, please. Please.

"Sharon Ryan?"

"No, no, that's not me." I was beginning to hyperventilate.

"Oh! Wait! Mr. Sweet just walked in. Let me see if he'll take the call." She put me on hold and I thought, *Of course he'll take the call, you idiot!* But it was her voice, not his, that came on the line. She sighed again. "I'm sorry. I was correct the first time. Mr. Sweet isn't taking any new clients at this time. Would you like to speak with one of the associates?"

"I told you before! I am not a new client!" My voice ricocheted inside the Jeep. My ears throbbed. "Please," I whimpered. "You've got to believe me. He's my lawyer, for God's sake. Okay?"

For a moment I thought I heard my answer back, thought I heard her say "Okay." Then I realized that it was the echo of my own voice, feedback from my stupid cell phone. The secretary had hung up. I had been talking to myself.

I sat in the car and fought back an overpowering fatigue, an almost primitive urge to go to sleep, to shut down, shut everything out. Roger was no longer at the doorway. I pulled out of the driveway and just started driving. I had no idea where I was going. I just knew I had to keep moving.

My cell phone rang. It was Roger. "I know you're in no mood to talk with me but I just wanted to remind you that I've got a rehearsal at two. You'll have to pick up Petey today. Okay?"

"Okay!" I snapped the phone shut.

I thought about Mary. That poor girl. What had Roger done to her? I had to contact that guy who runs Classy Ladies, tell him about Mary's disappearance. My skull was vibrating. I found myself outside Omar Sweet's office. I pulled into a visitor parking spot and ran inside. I punched the elevator button, decided I couldn't wait, took the stairs instead. I spotted the secretary right away, a frazzled-looking redhead with a silver ring in her eyebrow. "I'm here to see Omar Sweet, and I'm not leaving until I do."

She looked at me blandly and buzzed his line. "Mr. Sweet, Ms. Ryan is here to see you, and she says she refuses to leave until you talk with her." She looked at me again. "Have a seat. He'll be right out."

I felt triumphant. Now we were getting somewhere! "No, that's fine. I think I'll stand."

I heard a rustling down the corridor, the movement of Omar's swift, long legs. "Ms. Ryan?"

I turned toward the unfamiliar voice. He was a short, round man with greasy black hair. His shoulders were speckled with dandruff and I could smell his stale breath even from a distance. "Ms. Ryan?"

I figured it was one of his flunkies. "I'm here to see Omar, please."

The man extended a hand. "I'm Omar Sweet."

The last thing I remember was the pale watercolor on the wall behind his head, and the kelly green carpet, the way it felt against my cheek when my face hit the floor. When I opened my eyes, the secretary was holding something under my nose, a slice of lemon. I heard her whisper, "Look. It's working. She's coming to." The man with the greasy hair was propping me up, offering me a paper cup. "Have a little water. Are you okay?"

"Are you sure you're Omar Sweet?"

The man smiled warmly. "Last time I checked." He helped me to my feet.

"But the Omar Sweet I met was tall and . . . bald."

The man ran a hand through his hair. "No, I assure you Ms. Ryan, it's all mine."

I stared at him. "Look. Something terrible has happened. You don't understand. A man who called himself Omar Sweet was going to be my lawyer. He was supposed to serve my husband with divorce papers this morning. Tall, bald, silver goatee. Does he work here? You've got to tell me!"

I sounded like a lunatic and looked like hell. He had no reason to believe me. "Look. I've got to go." The man insisted I stay until I felt better, offered me coffee or a can of pop. But I had to help Mary. I had to get to the library. There were public computers there. I could go on-line, send an e-mail to that Prost guy, who ran CLIT.

I took a left on Bemble and now I was about a half mile from the library. The road was clear. If I didn't hit any red lights, I'd make it to the library in three minutes. Someone tried to cut into my lane. An old lady. I honked wildly. Get out of my way! But she scooted in front of me, then, naturally, slowed to a snail's pace. I checked my speedometer. I was now going eight miles an hour. Shit! I pulled up next to her and lowered my window. "Learn to drive, you batty old bitch!" I screamed out, watching my own spittle fly out the window. The woman turned to look at me. Jesus! It was Carla Schumann, Pete's first baby-sitter. A sweet, caring woman who said she thought of me as a daughter. I prayed she didn't recognize me and raced ahead.

The library was unusually crowded. I was afraid I might not get a computer, but I found an open one in the corner. I got on Netscape, quickly set up an e-mail account, typed in classyladiesinternationaltrade.com, and waited. I e-mailed H. Wilhem Prost, said I had reason to believe that harm has come to one of his "girls." I told him everything I knew, gave Roger's name, and asked him to write back ASAP.

I checked the e-mail account, and, miraculously, found a response from Prost: "Sorry, but I have no records of any CLIT girl interacting with anyone named Roger Tisdale. In fact, we haven't transacted any business with any gentlemen in your city. Good luck with your search. H. Wilhem Prost."

I left the library and started sprinting toward the Jeep. I couldn't run. My shins ached, and I got a stitch in my side. I felt weighted down, paralyzed. I couldn't breathe. I grabbed a parking meter for support and stood there, panting, crying. Passersby were staring. "What the hell are you staring at?" I screamed out. "Mind your own goddamn business!"

I wobbled back to the Jeep. I was suddenly filled with the most visceral need to be with Petey. Regardless of what happened with Roger, I would always have my son. My chest ached with yearning to hold my child, to smell his hair, kiss his fingers. It took twenty minutes to get to his school, and in that time I called my mother and Betsy, neither of whom were home. I felt so disconnected. It was an awful, alien feeling. Pete looked confused when I showed up at his classroom. He was afraid I'd come to take him to the doctor. I strapped him into his booster seat, and told him we were going to see Daddy's rehearsal.

I wasn't done with Roger. I had no idea what I would say to him, but there was no way I'd let him go about his business as if nothing had happened. I pulled up to the Dante Theater, and for the first time in my life, I parked in a handicapped spot. The lobby was locked, so Pete and I went to the back door, which was almost always open. A young woman strode several paces in front of me, her glossy black hair swinging as she walked. Oh, God. Could it be? I quickened my pace and called out to the girl. "Mary?"

Just as she turned around to face me, Petey started tugging my hand. I felt drugged, heavy, hot. I struggled to break through a kind of gelatinous barrier between me and the girl. I wanted to touch her, but she was always just out of reach. She smiled wickedly at me, pulled a wad of chewing gum from her mouth and popped it back in. Pete pulled my hand again, harder now. "Mom?"

"Not now, Pete," I muttered.

"Mom? Please."

With a rush of adrenaline and a feeling of relief so profound it made me weep, I realized I'd been dreaming. I wasn't backstage at the Dante, but in my own bed. That vivid feeling of the scratchy carpet against my cheek was the prickly embroidered decorative pillow I'd been too tired to toss off the bed. Roger was snoring, whistling through his nose, and I'd never been so grateful to hear his drone. It was three in the morning. The clock on the VCR was flashing like a strobe light (we never did figure out how to set it). I could hear the ice maker churning downstairs. Pete was at my side, rubbing his eyes. His pajama top was open and by the aquamarine light of the VCR clock, I could see a ghostly sheen of sweat on his bony chest.

"I had a bad dream" he whispered.

"Me too," I told him. "I had a bad dream too." I pulled him into bed and curled my arms around his waist. His hair was damp and smelled like baby shampoo. I squeezed him tighter. "Do you want to tell me about your dream?"

"No," he whispered back. His body softened in my arms, and soon I heard the deep, measured breathing of his sleep. As I held my son, I allowed myself to recall bits of the dream, gingerly reconstructing it from the few remaining shards. I tried to find the deeper meaning in that horrible nightmare, some higher purpose. Today I have the chance to expose a philandering husband, end a torturous marriage, begin anew with my child. But in my dream, I was going nowhere, completely stuck, completely alone. Why had I manufactured a dream in which the people I'd most depended upon—my lawyer, my investigator—were all shills in the service of my husband? And why, instead of divorce papers, did Roger hand me a photo of me in bed with my lover? I knew that dissecting the dream this way would dilute some of its power, but I was too tired now. I had a long day ahead of me and it was almost 4 A.M. Eventually I slipped back into a deep, dreamless sleep.

'Til next time,

𝒱

March 3

I didn't awaken until the alarm sounded at 7:30. I felt elated, and even found myself singing in the shower, "It was a dream, it was a dream, it was all a bad dream!"

Roger rapped on the pebbled door. "What are you so happy about?"

"I'm just glad to be awake!" I shouted over the roaring shower. "I'm thrilled to be alive and awake on this fine day!" I squirted blue Garden Musk shower gel on a sponge. I'd bought the stuff in desperation years ago, after I overheard someone at the store say it worked like an aphrodisiac on her husband. It hadn't had the same effect on Roger. In fact, he said it smelled like insecticide. I brought the soapy sponge to my nose and inhaled deeply. I thought it smelled like sex in the woods. I loved it.

I dropped Petey off at school and sped out to Lake Merle, as planned. I held my breath as I approached the house. What if my dream had been prophetic, and Mary had really packed up and left? Or what if there was no Mary after all? But before I even got out of the car, the door flew open and Mary was waving happily. "Mrs. Ryan! Mrs. Ryan!" I waved back at my new best friend. "I hoped you would come today," she yelled, "and here you are!"

She was wearing denim shorts and a black T-shirt I'd bought at Target years ago that bore the words: "I Fish, Therefore I Lie." I still don't know why I bought that shirt given the fact that I'd never been fishing. It had been among the things Roger said he'd take to Promise House. Mary's closet was probably filled with all the dreck I'd bought on impulse and never wore.

She pulled me inside. "Tippy had her babies!" She linked her arm in mine and led me past my ugly painting into the small kitchen. The condo smelled of fried food and Pine Sol. The cat, who lay in a cardboard Hammermill paper box, gazed up at me dully, while six tiny kittens nuzzled against her belly.

I took a deep breath. "Mary, I need to tell you something."

She squatted by the box and stroked the cat's head. "Do you want one of the babies?"

"No, honey, I don't. Listen, we need to talk. Now."

"Do you want some pop! Or tea?"

"Roger is my husband. And we've been married a long, long time." I watched her try to process this information.

"My Roger? Roger Tisdale? My husband?"

"Yes." I pulled out a picture from my wallet. It was my wedding picture.

She brought it up to her face and squinted at it. "Not my Roger. Mine's older. And not so fat."

I sighed. "That's what he looked like back then, Mary. He's older now. He lost weight. Believe me, it's him."

She shook her head and folded her arms across her chest. "Not him. Not possible."

I wished I had a more recent photograph. Then I remembered my key chain. I took it from my pocket and showed it to her. "Look at this, Mary." Encased in a Lucite oval was a photo of Roger and Pete last fall at the Tiger Cub camping trip.

Mary peered at it and smirked. "Still not him." I took another look at the picture and saw that my husband's face was bleached by a splash of sunlight. I knew it was him because, well, who else would it be? But I suppose from Mary's perspective—the perspective of someone whose identity as the wife of a "famous" American playwright now depends on refuting my claim—this man with the bleached-out face could be anyone.

I was starting to feel panicky. I had to get this girl back to my house before the deputy arrived. "Listen, Mary. Please. I know things about Roger that only a wife"—my throat tightened—"or a lover would know. Like, there's a red mark on his rear end shaped just like Texas." I realized she probably didn't know where Texas was, let alone the shape of it, so I found a pen in my bag and drew a picture on the back of a bank deposit slip. "Here. Like this." Mary stared at it but said nothing.

I went on. "A wife would know that his favorite breakfast is vanilla yogurt with granola and a glass of apricot nectar, and his second favorite is a banana-nut bagel with honey-walnut cream cheese. And a wife would know that he times it so that he finishes the bagel and his coffee—black, no sugar—at exactly the same time." I checked Mary's expression. Her eyes looked watery, but otherwise her face remained stony.

"Let's see . . ." I continued. "He pees in spurts, and sometimes it sounds like he's peeing out a song, like 'Mary Had A Little Lamb'—you know, pee pee pee pee pee-pee-pee. Wait. I know. He's afraid of bees, he hates Swiss cheese, he only brushes his teeth *after* he eats breakfast because he doesn't like how food tastes with toothpaste in his mouth, and oh! the little toe of his left foot is weird, like this." I quickly slipped off my shoe and crossed my pinky toe over the next toe. "See?"

No reaction.

I was sweating now. "And he just loves *Xena*. If *Xena*'s on, forget it. Nothing else matters." I knew this was a long shot. In all likelihood, he was too busy screwing this girl to watch *Xena* or anything else on the tube. Surely his devotion to *Xena* was a by-product of his boredom with me, but I threw it out there anyway.

Bingo! Mary's face crumpled and she sobbed into her hands. I heard her whimper, "Yes. *Xena*. How I hate that lady!"

I moved closer and put an arm around her. It would have been so easy to hate her, but my heart ached for this girl. "Listen, sweetheart, Roger played a bad trick on you. Can you understand that?" She howled louder. "He's a bad man. He already has a wife. Me. And he has a little boy. See?" I took out the key chain again and held it in front of Mary's face. She peeked at it from between her fingers. "It's Petey. He's just a little boy. Such a sweet little boy. And Roger is his father."

Mary stopped crying and started snorting mucus back into her throat. Her nose was red and bulbous. It was getting late. I had to move quickly now. "Look, Mary, Roger is not allowed to have more than one wife. It's illegal. Do you understand what that means? It's against the law."

Her eyes widened. "Am I going to be in trouble? With the policemen?"

I had her now. She was scared. "I don't know, Mary. Maybe." I hated to exploit her gullibility, but what choice did I have? "People in this country aren't allowed to have two wives at the same time. And if you lied about your age, well, that's also against the law."

She was crying again. I stroked her hair. "Mary, I'm going to help you, I swear. We're going to straighten everything out and I'm going to make sure you don't get put in jail or anything. But now you have to come with me. Okay?"

She nodded. "Okay. I'll come." She was barefoot. I grabbed the flip-flops by the door and handed them to her.

Mary stared out of the Jeep's window all the way home, and I realized that this was all new to her, these streets filled with gas stations, chain restaurants, and Laundromats. Roger had kept her a prisoner; he'd convinced her that the condominium was all the world she would ever need. I knew that I'd attained the highest level of detachment from Roger when I realized that I cared more about this girl's welfare than the fact that she'd had sex with my husband. As I sped down Market Street Mary would occasionally lapse into sobs, and I'd reach out to pat her arm. "You poor little thing," I told her. "We're going to make things right, I promise."

I can't begin to describe the warmth that flooded my veins as I neared the house. Everything was going according to plan. I had Mary. In less than an hour, the divorce papers would be in Roger's hands. If Omar does his job, I'm going to be a wealthy woman and Roger will be destitute. I felt the purest joy, an excitement so powerful I thought I might shatter.

I pulled into the garage and instructed Mary to stay put. Roger was upstairs. It was now 11:30. I grabbed a canister of Pringle's, some Little Debbie zebra cakes, a can of diet Coke and brought it back to the Jeep. "It may be a while. Do you want anything else?"

Mary tore into one of the Little Debbie cakes and took a bite. "You have any magazines?"

I raced back into the house and found a stack of *People* and *Entertainment Weekly* in the family room. Her eyes lit up when she saw the magazines. "Oooh! The Backstreet Boys!" She released a small smile. "Thank you."

I left her alone with the junk food and magazines and prayed they would keep her busy for a while. I used my remote to lock the Jeep doors. If she tried to escape, the alarm would sound.

Then the doorbell rang. I glanced outside and saw the sheriff's car. I called upstairs. "Roger, can you please get the door? I'm in the bathroom." I scooted into the bathroom and listened as Roger trotted downstairs and swung open the front door.

"Roger Tisdale?" a deep voice boomed.

"Yes, that's me." Roger's voice was thin, wary.

"This is for you, sir. Thank you, sir." The door closed; the lock clicked. I stepped outside the bathroom just as Roger was surveying the envelope. His face was gray. I froze in the bathroom doorway as Roger fingered the envelope.

"A sheriff's deputy just delivered this," he said quietly. "It looks like it's from a law firm."

This is it, I told myself. It's happening. It's really happening. I wanted to jump out of my skin. I fought to keep my voice even. "Aren't you going to open it?"

Roger slumped in a chair by the kitchen table. "I'm afraid to."

"What are you afraid of, Roger?" I was sure he knew. I was wrong.

He stared at me. "I'm just afraid it's another, you know, another lawsuit. An Alyssa thing. You know."

Oh dear. Poor Roger had apparently gotten himself into another mess. I decided to play with him. "Well, maybe you'd better tell me about it before you open that envelope."

His head sagged into his hands. "Sweet Jesus!" he cried melodramatically. "Why me? Why must it always be me?"

"Come on now, Roger, why don't you tell me about it? It can't be that bad."

"Oh yes, I'm afraid it can." Apparently Roger had taken a "special interest" in one of his actresses, the girl with the body piercings who had once delivered pizza to our house. Now he fears that his interest might have been "misinterpreted." She'd quit the cast two weeks ago, hinted that she was getting a lawyer. "But I swear, I never touched the girl. I swear!"

"Oh, Roger, it must be so hard to be you." He looked at me and bobbed his head. "A man of such passion such creativity. And so misunderstood!"

"Yes, yes, that's exactly it!" he cried. "You know me so well!"

"Now why don't you go ahead and open the envelope? Just get it over with," I urged.

He gazed at me gratefully. "As long as I have you on my side."

"Of course, Roger. Now open it."

He slipped a finger behind the flap and slid it along the length of the envelope. He slowly unfolded the letter, took a deep breath, and began to read. "What the hell . . . ?" he looked stupefied. "What is this?"

"I'm leaving you, Roger. It's over. I'm divorcing you." Oh, the sheer joy of finally pronouncing those words!

"But why?" he shrieked. "Why?"

"There are many reasons, Roger. And my attorney will be happy to detail them for you. But the most important reason is a young girl named Mary."

"Who?" he asked, as I'd hoped he would.

I started toward the garage. "Don't move, darling husband. I'll be right back."

When I got back to the Jeep, Mary was sound asleep (knocked out by all the junk food, no doubt, a condition with which I am intimately familiar). I used the remote to unlock the doors; the loud click woke her up. She blinked at me and stretched. "Can I go in now, Mrs. Ryan?" She lowered her voice. "I have to pee."

"Absolutely, sweetheart. But first, we need to talk to Roger. See, just like I thought, he says he doesn't know you. He's lying again. And we need to help him see the truth. Do you understand that?"

She nodded at me. "I understand, Mrs. Ryan." I helped her out of the Jeep and tightened my grip on her soft, slender arm. I couldn't risk her running away, not when we were this close to blowing up Roger's life.

As I steered her toward the door that leads from the garage to the family room, I surveyed all the junk piled in corners and on the wooden shelves, the artifacts of our life together. Actually, they're more like artifacts of the life we never led. The matching Rollerblades we bought when one of our marriage counselors told us we needed to play together more. (We used them twice.) The unopened cans of periwinkle paint I bought when I read about the healing power of color and decided that what our marriage really needed was a fresh coat of paint. The canoe and helmets we bought for what Roger promised would be a lifetime of outdoor adventure. We'd driven out to Quetico Provincial Park in Canada. Roger sprained his hand attempting to wrench the canoe off the roof of the car, then spent the next three days whining about it. That was the last canoe trip we ever took. Let me amend that: It was my last canoe trip. How many girls he seduced on the banks of Gunflint Lake is anyone's guess.

I held Mary's hand as we walked into the family room. As I approached the kitchen I called out, "To

answer your question, Roger . . ." I gently pushed
Mary through the archway dividing the family room
from the kitchen. "Heeeeere's Mary!" I felt intoxi-
cated. I was floating so high above this man, he was
now a dark speck in the vast aerial view of my life. I
watched him as Mary stepped tentatively into the
room. Roger tightly wrapped his arms around himself, as if to prevent some involuntary confession or
gesture of recognition. He looked at her face. Actually, he seemed to focus on a spot above her head. He
never looked into her eyes.

Mary raced toward him and threw herself at his
feet, humbly and adoringly, like one of those little
kids in *The King and I.* "Is true what Mrs. Ryan says,
Roger? Is true that she's your real wife? Is true?"

Roger looked down at the girl. "Get the hell off
me!" he yelled. Then he hit her with his loafer, not a
kick exactly, more like an attempt to pry her off his
legs.

She started to cry. "Why are you doing this, my
husband? Don't you know who I am? Your little
Mary! Don't you remember me? I'm your wife, your
little love blossom!"

Roger looked at me. "Who the hell is this person?"
Roger seemed sincerely confused. Suddenly I wasn't
so giddy anymore. I was scared. Had I made some
bizarre mistake? Was Mary part of some elaborate
scam designed to humiliate me?

I continued. "Don't bullshit me, Roger. You know

exactly who this is, and so do I, and so does my private investigator." I helped Mary to her feet and held her as she sobbed and snorted into my chest. "You make me sick," I said.

"You make me sicker," he shouted, hoisting himself onto his all-too-familiar high horse. I could see him inflate with self-righteousness as he warmed to his new strategy: He would take the offensive. "You bring this girl into our house from God knows where, and you believe whatever craziness she tells you. Who knows what she has in mind, what she plans to steal from this house, what diseases she's carrying! You put your family and home in jeopardy all because some wacko tells you she's my wife? You're the sick one, my dear." He twirled a finger at his temple. "Certifiably loony!"

Now Mary was howling. I forged ahead. "Did you really think you were going to get away with this, Roger? You're a smart man. What on earth made you think you could have some kind of crazy pseudo secret marriage with a sixteen-year-old girl and actually get away with it?"

Roger jumped up and pointed an accusing finger at Mary. "You said you were twenty-one."

All three of us gasped at Roger's self-revelatory faux pas. He covered his mouth with a hand and fell back in the chair. "Dear God," he muttered. "Dear God."

I stared at him. "You pathetic excuse for a man.

You depraved, decripit sicko. You make me want to vomit."

Roger rubbed his eyes wearily. "Don't let me stop you," he answered. "But not on the carpet, please." I marveled at his ability, even in his ravaged state, to construct a snide comeback.

"Allow me to enumerate your crimes," I said. "Number one, you're a bigamist. In case you're wondering, bigamy is prohibited in our state, according to Statute 1846, which states, in Section Five, 'No marriage shall be contracted whilst either of the parties has a former wife or husband living, unless the marriage with such former wife or husband shall have been dissolved.'" He stared at me and I beamed back. "I looked it up on the Internet!" I was feeling giddy again. "Number two, you're probably going to be convicted of statutory rape!"

"I think not," Roger said. "The legal age of consent in this state is sixteen. *I* looked it up on the Internet." He thrust his chin out defiantly.

"But I was only fifteen when we started," Mary said quietly.

Roger and I looked at her. Roger put his hands over his face. "Jesus God."

I looked at my watch. "You have twenty minutes to pack a bag. Call me with your address and I'll have the rest of your crap sent to you tomorrow. Just get the hell out of here."

Roger stood up and wagged a finger at me. "You're

not going to get away with this, you realize that."
Roger was up to his neck in his own shit and he's still
playing the aggrieved one. I could hear him stomping
around upstairs like a kid who has lost his video game
privileges. Doors were slammed, drawers were flung
open and banged shut. I heard him punch the wall
and scream, "Fuck! Fuck! She can't do this to me!"

Mary looked frightened. "What's he gonna do to
us, Mrs. Ryan?"

I held her in my arms. Her hair smelled of Alberto
VO5. "He's never going to do anything to either of
us, ever again."

She started sobbing. "It's just not fair, Mrs. Ryan."

"What's not fair, Mary?"

"I was supposed to be a married American wife.
That's what I was supposed to be!"

Mary seemed to be teetering between heartbreak
and an aggressive sense of entitlement, the way Pete
gets when he's denied something he'd expected to
have. ("But you *told* me the ice cream truck would
come through the neighborhood today! It's just not
fair!") I didn't know what to say except the lame, all-
purpose: "Nobody ever said life was going to be fair."

She looked up at me and blinked. "True." She
hugged me more tightly now.

"Thank you, Mrs. Ryan. Thank you for being my
friend."

I had no idea what I was going to do with a
sixteen-year-old Filipina, but I certainly didn't plan

to send her back to that cell on Lake Merle. I told her I'd pay for her way back to the Philippines. "Oh no, Mrs. Ryan!" She was terrified. "I can't ever go back home. My father would kill me if he found out what happened. I can't ever go back, ever. Please don't send me back there!"

"Mary, do you have any family in the States?"

She bit her lip and nodded. "Somewhere in Philadelphia." She pronounced it "Pilladelphia." "They are cousins of my father."

"Mary, I'm going to try to arrange for you to live with them. Until then"—I swallowed hard—"you can stay with me for a while, me and Pete."

She was elated. "And Tippy? With the babies?"

"Well, Tippy yes, but we'll have to bring the babies to the animal shelter. We can't take them too."

"Okay, Mrs. Ryan. That's okay." She looked disappointed, but quickly brightened. "Thank you, Mrs. Ryan."

"Call me Valerie, please." Suddenly I heard the door slam and I knew Roger was leaving. The garage door rumbled open. Mary and I went to the bay window in the living room and we watched his van back out of the driveway. His eyes met mine as he pulled away. Then he flashed his middle finger.

Mary is in the guest room now, watching *I Love Lucy*. It's been a long day.

'Til next time,

V

March 4

Mary's period is eleven days late. This morning she threw up after breakfast. I should be ripping my hair out, but I feel oddly serene. Is it the Prozac, or the prospect of having a baby in the house again? I know the neighbors would relish the gossip: First my husband had an underage lover, and now a baby? But the compelling reality is that this child would be linked by blood to my own son. Why wouldn't I want that child growing up in this house? On the other hand, the baby would be a constant reminder of Roger's sexual hubris. And what if Roger insists on helping to raise this child? On the other, other hand: A baby! A sweet, soft package of cuddly love! I get all gooey inside just thinking about it. Or am I just losing my mind?

'Til next time,

𝒱

March 4, continued

Oh, God. Mary says that she wants to "make the baby go away." Apparently, Roger phoned her while I was out and insisted she get an abortion or he would get her booted out of the country. She's been on the phone all afternoon with her Auntie Esta in the Philippines. From what I can piece together, Esta belongs to some kind of underground women's group that, among other services, dispenses advice on do-it-yourself abortion.

"Auntie Esta knows everything," Mary told me. She waved a paper in front of my face. In the bubbly universal handwriting of teen girls, Mary had scribbled a list of herbs. I recognized a few. Black cohosh. Pennyroyal. "Please," she begged. "We got to go to the store."

I grabbed the paper and ripped it up. "Roger lied to you," I told her, shouting over her sobs. "He's a liar, Mary. Don't you realize that by now? Nobody is throwing you out of the country." I told her that I would arrange for her citizenship. I told her everything would be okay, though I didn't quite believe it myself.

'Til next time,

V

March 5

Dale called this morning, just when I was yanking Petey out of bed. I picked up the phone. "Hello?"

"How many surrealists does it take to screw in a lightbulb?"

My heart did a little flip-flop of joy. Dale, a social worker and my closest friend when I worked at the Center, one of the few people who knew me in my former life. Dale knew me when I wore stockings and high heels, when I carried a briefcase and earned my own money.

"I don't know, Dale. How many surrealists does it take to screw in a lightbulb?"

"Fish." He paused, waited for me to laugh. I did. "Hey," he continued, "did you hear the one about the dyslexic-agnostic insomniac? He stays up all night wondering if there really is a Dog."

I immediately felt lighter and happier. It turns out Dale finally quit the Center. "Too much bureaucratic bullshit," he said.

"So what are you going to do next?"

"Well, Eric and I were thinking of moving out to Vermont to get married, except I can't stand those snooty New Englanders. So I guess we'll just stay here and pretend we're brothers so our upstanding neighbors keep liking us."

"You're not serious. You and Eric pretend you're brothers?"

"We do! We say we're twins, fraternal, which explains why we don't look alike."

"Which explains why he's black?"

Dale laughed. "Well, the truth is, we don't really talk to the neighbors, which is fine by me. They're all so icky."

"So you might as well move to Vermont. At least you won't have to pretend you're brothers."

"Maybe. Anyway, enough about me. What's up with you?"

While Petey brushed his teeth, I gave Dale a quick sketch: Eddie, Diana, Roger's pathological infidelity, Dad's illness, Mary, the divorce.

"Oh, sweetie, that's a heavy load for one lifetime. How do you find the motivation to get out of bed in the morning?"

"It's called Prozac," I told him.

"Hey, welcome to the club."

"You too?" I asked, feeling like we were sharing a sly secret.

"Yes, ma'am. Every day for the last nine months. Wouldn't skip a dose if you paid me."

"Oh, Dale, it's so good to hear your voice. I've missed you."

"Likewise, my friend, likewise." We made plans to get together for lunch next week, then it was time to get Pete to school. "By the way," he added, "I've got very juicy news about our old friend."

"Who?"

"Marissa, Clarissa, whatever her name was. The hooker."

"Oh, God. Tell me!"

"No. Not now. Next week. Over lunch," he said. "This way you can't cancel out on me."

Later, after Pete was down for the night, I tried to explain my feelings about abortion to Mary, feelings that have always been more visceral than political, which is why I hesitate to share them. I don't think most people would peg me for the anti-abortion type; I mean, it's not like I'd ever stand in front of Planned Parenthood with a picket sign. Actually, it was my sister Teresa who prodded me into finally crystallizing my thoughts on the topic. We were in the kitchen, and I'd spotted some ants marching across the counter. Roger would have crushed them under his thumb, but I felt compelled to herd them into a Dixie cup and release them outside. I did the same with mice, moths, beetles, even roaches.

"Lemme get this straight, little sister," Teresa said. "You don't have the heart to kill a tiny sugar ant, but killing a developing person is okay?" I didn't want to debate her because I knew I'd lose, but her comment stuck. And once I became pregnant with Pete, I became even more ambivalent about abortion.

I dug up a book of photos taken inside the womb, the one I read practically every day when I was pregnant with Pete. As Mary and I flipped through the pages, I thought: This is Mary's body, not mine. Mary's pregnancy, not mine. Mary's choice, not mine. But I couldn't have lived with myself if I hadn't at least tried to offer a different perspective. I think she has changed her mind. She hasn't asked about the herbs, hasn't called her Aunt Esta. So I think we're okay. For now.

'Til next time,

V

March 6

I just had some film developed, which means it's time once again to confront the issue of my weight. The first few shots were taken over a year ago, when I was exercising daily, sometimes even twice a day, and eating Lean Cuisines every night. It was around the time I'd first met Ben on the StairMaster, and I remembered how confident I'd felt in my black flared stretch pants and tight white cap-sleeved cotton T-shirts.

Toward the end of the roll were the pictures Pete had snapped a few nights ago as I prepared dinner. Only a year had passed, but I appeared ten years older. My arms were twin dolphins, my face an over-ripe melon. As Pete happily pawed through the prints, I felt only shame. What had happened? Why had I lost the zeal to keep my body lithe and fit? A year ago, clothes shopping was a pleasurable experience. I could wear black stretch capri pants. I felt comfortable in shorts and swimsuits. I'd see slim women and include myself in their elite club, a club whose members can unselfconsciously wear sleeveless tops and short skirts and clingy matte jersey. Acquaintances stopped me on the street just to say, You look fantastic! Or, What's your secret? A neighbor who had just begun working out confessed that I'd been her inspiration.

What would those admirers think now? I've quietly tucked away the black capri stretch pants and all the rest of the small-sized clothes and remorsefully calculate the money I spent on my new body, the body I'm apparently not destined to have. I find myself searching through my closet for oversized stretch pants with elastic waistbands. There are angry red marks where my pants and bra straps cut into my flesh. How can I contemplate dating again, disrobing in front of a man, letting him wrap his arms around my waist? Intellectually, of course, I believe that everyone has a right to a relationship, regardless of size or shape. My mother and her neighbors used to cluck over married women who had let themselves "go to pot." Mom had restricted her calories through every pregnancy, and never gained more than fifteen pounds with each baby, as she is fond of reminding me. I once found her weeping in her bedroom—I was sure my father had died in a car accident on the way home from work. It turned out that she had gained three and a half pounds.

I find it impossible to accept my body as it is now that I've seen those pictures. Somewhere at the margins of consciousness, in that murky place beyond the tranquilizing effects of medication, I feel the purest disgust for my body. I find the prospect of starting from square one daunting and depressing. I dread starting again with the rigorous workouts, the tiny meals. Weighing, measuring, calorie calculating. . .

Motivation is magical and elusive. I had it once. I've got to get it back. To hell with self-acceptance. If Prozac is to blame for any of this—and my doctor says it may be—then I'm through with Prozac. I'd rather be crazy than fat.

'Til next time,

V

March 7

Roger called with a news bulletin. He crunched the numbers and came to the conclusion that even with alimony, I can't possibly live in the manner to which I have grown accustomed. "Face it, Valerie," he declared. "You can't afford to live without my income. You'll be pushing all your worldly belongings through town in a shopping cart by the time Pete's in third grade." I shuddered. "So forget about the divorce," he continued. "Let's make our marriage work." I hung up on him and disconnected the phone.

Omar is scheduled to take Roger's deposition tomorrow. I can't wait to see what Roger concocts about his assets. I hope he lies, I really do, because the less money he claims to have, according to Omar, the larger a settlement I'm likely to get.

'Til next time,

V

March 8

Roger's deposition went exactly as Omar had hoped. My soon-to-be ex-husband insisted under oath that he had no assets other than the trust fund, the income from his theater projects, the little bit he has made teaching, and our joint holdings: the house, vehicles, material possessions. Roger made no mention of Swiss or Cayman bank accounts, paintings, cash, or gold. He didn't even name the condo on Lake Merle. Now Omar plans to argue that because Roger lied under oath, and given his criminal history—sexual harassment, statutory rape, bigamy—I am entitled to not merely half, but *all* of his hidden assets. I still can't believe the court would swallow this reasoning, but Omar's confidence is unshakable. "This is my job, love," he said, and I felt my cheeks flush. "You relax and let me do the work."

"Okay, fine. You do the work. Just wake me up when it's all over, okay?"

'Til next time,

V

March 9

I've been fantasizing about leaving town, finding some place way on the other side of the world where Pete and I can make a new life, and not just so I can escape Roger and his current blastocyst. There are so many things about this place that I find increasingly intolerable. I offer four examples:

1. The Mushroomheads—by which I mean the Junior Leaguers, the ones who pop up everywhere in their white Ford Excursions or whatever those gigantic new SUVs are called. (I've decided, by the way, that my next vehicle will have to be a semi, because I'm sick of being dwarfed on the road, and no one could possibly top an eighteen-wheeler.) Three Mushroomheads walk the track at the gym every day. They always walk three-across (flagrantly disregarding the two-across limit), with their three identically highlighted blond heads coifed in identical mushroom-shaped hairdos, three tiny behinds, three pert noses, three walnut-size diamonds on their French-manicured fingers. (I had my fake nails removed, by the way; I noticed a tremor in my left pinkie and decided, in an intensely neurotic moment, that the acrylic was seeping into my blood and would eventually cause Parkinson's disease. I realized only after I'd had them removed that the tremor was from using the weed whacker for ninety relentless minutes, a feat I accomplished only by imagining that the pigweed was Roger's genitalia.)

2. The claustrophobia—by which I mean I feel like I can't go anywhere without banging into someone I know. At a four-way stop last week, I realized I knew the drivers at the other three stop signs. There'd

been an accident at the intersection of Ridge and 16th streets, and I knew both drivers. I was at Pak-Mail and happened to glance down into the trash can, where I noticed a manila envelope addressed to Leanne Swanson. I know Leanne Swanson. She was in my Lamaze class when I was pregnant with Pete. Roger liked to flirt with her. Then one day she farted when we were practicing pushing—not just a meek little toot but a thick, juicy, cheese-cutter. Roger didn't flirt with Leanne Swanson after that.

3. The Stonehenge Syndrome—by which I mean the bizarre compulsion townsfolk have to display small versions of Stonehenge (or similarly stark configurations of roughhewn stone columns) on front lawns. I do not understand this. In other places, people seem to do just fine with statues of saints, or concrete ducks, or those flat wooden things that are meant to look like a little fat person in bloomers bent over picking strawberries.

4. The dearth of good Chinese restaurants—by which I mean that what passes for Chinese food here would make most people recoil in horror. Our Chinese restaurants serve white bread. Enough said.

But just when I am sure I can't possibly tolerate another day here, I realize I have nowhere else to go. My parents are here. My grandparents and great-grandparents are buried here. I went to a church potluck last week and felt affection for everyone, even the people who annoy me, like crotchety Pearlie

Wilson, who never smiles and who sneaks leftovers into her straw bag when she thinks no one's looking. Or Mel Ruckbaker, who's always trying to sucker someone into one of his get-rich-quick schemes. There's Chad Weaver, all peach fuzz and acne, trying to catch a glimpse of Tiffany Campbell's breasts as she leans over the punch bowl. I see Reverend Lee offer a welcoming handshake to that young couple who just moved here from New York City, and I hear him assure them that we may not be as exciting as the Big Apple, but this is a heck of a great place to raise kids. They smile politely, but they have no idea what he means, and they won't until they start raising kids here—and then they'll know exactly what the Reverend meant, and eventually they'll wonder why everyone makes such a big deal about New York—until someone serves them white bread in a Chinese restaurant.

'Til next time,

V

March 10

Had lunch with Dale today. The big news about Roger's young protegée is this: She's writing a tell-all book about her escapades as a coed hooker. And there's going to be a fat chapter on Roger, who, rumor has it, is described as a "saggy, sour-assed, washed-up hack writer."

I've slowly started telling people about my divorce. The reaction has been generally supportive. It's an amazing experience, actually—all these people I barely know confessing that they never liked Roger in the first place. The widow who lives at the end of the cul-de-sac approached me as I was pulling the trash cans to the curb. I froze in fear when I saw her. I thought she was going to yell at me about my trash cans, loitering at the curb like a couple of grungy hobos long after everyone else on the block has stowed theirs neatly and out of sight. "I just want you to know that I'm pulling for you. I never liked him, you know." She squeezed my arm and smiled benevolently. "You're better off without him, dear."

I wanted to say, You have lived here for seven years and I don't even know your name. "Thanks," I said.

I ran into Ben Murphy at the bank. He casually asked how I'd been.

"I'm divorced!" I blurted out. How did I expect him to react? Twirl me around and sing out in joyful gratitude? Actually, yes.

Instead he smiled (I like to think it was a wry, knowing, eager smile) and said, "Is that so?"

I returned the smile. "Yes, that's so."

"Well, then."

I waited but he didn't say anything else.

'Til next time,

Q

March 10, continued

Roger won't leave me alone. He called three times to-day. As soon as I see his name on Caller ID, I let the machine pick up. But the last time he called he used a pay phone, and I answered, damn it.

He says he has one final offer for me, and he's "absolutely convinced" that I'll be interested. I didn't have the strength to argue with him. I told him he could stop by tomorrow morning. For ten minutes. And that's it.

'Til next time,

V

March 11

When Roger showed up at the door this morning he looked far too hopeful for a man bound for divorce and, in all probability, jail. He carried a storage box, much like the one in which Tippy nursed her kittens. I glanced out the back window. Mary was sunning herself on a blanket in the yard while Pete darted in and out of the sprinkler.

"What have you got there, Roger?"

He smiled. "Patience, my dear." He nodded toward the kitchen. "May I?"

I stepped aside and let him through. "Go ahead."

He hefted the box onto the table and pushed it toward me. "Okay, kiddo, here's the deal."

"Whatever you're selling, *kiddo*, I'm not buying, so don't bother," I told him.

"I'm not selling a thing, wifey. I'm giving it away." He gestured toward the box with a flourish. "Go ahead. Open it."

"Don't call me wifey."

"I know you thought you could claim this as your own, and that's fine. I ask no questions, make no accusations. It's yours. Spend it however you'd like." He lifted the lid. "On one condition."

It was the strongbox. So it was Roger who'd ripped my parents' home apart, not Eddie.

"Condition, Roger?"

"Please abandon this silly divorce business and let us be a family again. I'm begging you."

He had to be kidding. Then again, he was just being Roger, a man whose capacity to lie to his wife was outweighed only by his capacity to lie to himself. Roger didn't realize that I knew he was worth far more than the contents of that box.

"You can't buy me back, Roger. Please take your lousy gold and go home." I tried to move him toward the door. He was rooted to the floor. He asked if he could see Pete. I blocked his view of the back window and told him that Pete was at Hunter's house. "Next time you need to contact me, call my attorney. I'm serious."

He winced. "Did Mary get rid of the baby as I'd suggested?"

"Get out of here, Roger." I wish I could expunge him from my life completely, but I know that as long as we have a child between us, I will have to deal with Roger, at some level, for another fifteen years or so, and I find this fact unbelievably depressing. I'd like to think I'd get full custody and he'd be denied visitation rights, but Omar has warned me that custody rulings in this state have been increasingly favorable toward men, even those with checkered histories. Some guy was granted visitation rights even though the child he was visiting was the product of acquaintance rape—he was the rapist.

'Til next time,

V

March 12

Speaking relatively, today was perfect. In the morning, I took Mary and Pete to church. Mary wasn't familiar with the liturgy, but she seemed completely connected to the services, enchanted by the music, riveted to Reverend Lee's sermon (topic: is it serendipity or divine intervention?). After church we went out for bagels (Mary had two), then hit the mall, where I bought her three pairs of shoes and let her go wild at Claire's, that girly doodads place in the mall.

Then the three of us squeezed into one of those little photo booths. When the picture slid out of the slot, Mary grabbed it and kissed it. "My family," she said.

It was a pleasure to watch her act like a real teenager, and I wondered whether it was a mistake to want her to go through the pregnancy.

According to today's paper, the *Heirloom Roadshow*—those earnest and overweight traveling antique experts—are coming to town. Lynette wants to go, and she wants me to come with her. "Come on, Val, it'll be a kick," she said excitedly. "I've been dying to get an expert opinion on my grandmother's old plates."

At first I demurred—I couldn't imagine a worse way to spend a Saturday afternoon, packed inside the mildewed National Guard armory with hundreds of locals and all their dusty old junk. Then I remembered my rapidly dwindling checking account. But what would I sell? My family wasn't big on heirlooms—my mother had given me her old Corelle plastic dinnerware when I got my first apartment and a cheap silver bracelet her grandfather gave her on her sixteenth birthday. Typical. My family has successfully slashed and burned all its geneological ties. Lynette had traced her own roots back to the Civil War. A couple of years ago, my sister Teresa made a halfhearted effort to trace our family history and came up with a potato farmer named Seamus.

"You could bring that sculpture, the one Roger

gave you for your birthday," Lynette suggested. "Didn't he tell you it was in his family for generations?"

I'd forgotten about that sculpture, a bronze cowboy affair I kept on the mantel. Roger hinted that the piece was extremely valuable. In fact, he said it once belonged to Franklin Roosevelt. If it was worth a few thousand dollars, it would cover my bills for a couple of months in a crunch.

'Til next time,

V

March 14

Yesterday morning I brought a breakfast tray into Mary's room but her room was empty. I reflexively looked under the bed—a child's hiding place—and while I didn't find Mary, I did discover a crumpled supermarket bag. Inside, brown glass bottles and a sticky teaspoon. Tinctures and oils, and a Ziploc bag of something that looked like tea. I recognized the names on the labels. These were the herbs Mary had asked me to buy for her, the herbs she thought would end her pregnancy.

I had a terrible premonition, the absolutely certain sense that Mary was in danger. I left Petey with Lynette and drove wildly through the streets, screaming Mary's name. I went as far north as Mercer, as far west as the highway. Mary was a strong girl. She could have been anywhere. Sweating, crying, desperate, I drove home and searched the house again, the basement, the attic. I stumbled outside, and something pulled me toward the ravine behind the house, a tangle of brush and trees, weeds, timber, and flat rock. I shuddered as I looked into its depth. Mary was down there, puking into the creek. She was wearing my old "I Fish, Therefore I Lie" T-shirt.

I yelled for help. Lynette ran onto the deck in her pajamas. I told her to call an ambulance. By 10 A.M., Mary was in the hospital having her stomach pumped. By 11:03, her kidneys had shut down. At 11:09, Mary was pronounced dead.

When I got home, I found her Aunt Esta's phone number by the phone in Mary's bedroom. She was stunned when I told her Mary was dead.

"What the hell is wrong with you?" I demanded. "Didn't you know those herbs could kill her?"

Esta then confessed that she knew virtually nothing about herbs. Her "specialty," she said, was tae kwon do. She said she found the herb information in an old handbook lying around the house. She said she had only wanted to help her niece.

I told her that I would arrange for Mary's body to be sent back to the Philippines, and she promised that she would accompany the casket from Manila to Ilocos, even though it meant facing Mary's parents. "This is all my fault, and I will tell them that," she said. "I take full responsibility."

I asked Esta to tell me everything she knew about Mary, and she did. I spent the hour listening to where this young girl had been, where she'd come from, and how she'd become my husband's other wife.

Mary was of the Ifugao people, industrious, clannish farmers known for engineering magnificent rice terraces in the steep Luzon Mountains. Her kin were among the poorest in the hamlet, and they subsisted primarily on the sweet potatoes they farmed on a small hillside plot; potatoes, and the meager cash they earned selling chickens for ritual sacrifice. Her parents planned to marry her off to the youngest son of a more prestigious family of rice farmers when she was twelve.

In the year of her twelfth birthday, Mary befriended a sociologist from Berkeley, a graduate student who had come to Hapau to study the microeconomy of Ifugao weavers. Mary convinced the student, the earnest daughter of a minister, to take her along to Manila, where Mary had a distant cousin. The student dropped her off at a post office, as Mary had requested. But the cousin never arrived, and Mary lived on the streets, panhandling with the other street kids. She was clever and hardworking, and became skilled at scrounging food in the trash bins behind restaurants. She made no attempt to contact her family in the mountains.

Two years later, a friend introduced her to H. Wilhem Prost, an enterprising American who said he had a way for poor girls to find happiness and security in the United States. When he said he ran a mail-order bride business, Mary balked—she'd heard about girls who were unwittingly "sold" into the sex industry—but Prost assured her he wasn't actually selling girls, just making introductions. "The men aren't buying you, silly," he said. "They're paying for the privilege of meeting you. It's all very legal. Romantic, even." Prost gave her a good Christian name, put her up in a cramped apartment over a Laundromat with four other young women, and gave them enough money to cover their expenses. Mary was grateful for the shelter and food.

Against enormous odds given the tightly woven fabric of the Ifugao community and the dominance of its patriarchy, Mary had made her way to Manila, traded her native Austronesian tongue for English, and became one of Prost's CLIT girls, posing in a chaste white starched shirt for his catalog. She'd lied about her age, and he pretended to believe her. Within two weeks of posting her photo online, Mary had her first offer, from a man who said he was a famous American playwright. He courted her by mail, sent her pictures of his home (*my house!*) and photocopies of newspaper reviews of his play, *Basic Black*. One of her roommates helped her translate the letters, and they were beautiful, poetic. But

Mary was frightened and she decided to abandon the whole scheme. The other girls prevailed, urged her to take the risk. They said that Mr. Tisdale seemed like a nice man. Besides, she wasn't compelled to marry him, just meet him. What would be the harm?

Once Mary made it to America, Roger insisted that she had no choice but to marry him. He told her she would live like a princess, that she would want for nothing. When she hesitated, he changed his approach. He told her that what she had done was illegal, and that the American government had special jails for girls like her. Mary was as gullible as Roger was convincing, and over time she decided she would have to make the best of it. She learned to like the pale American who disappeared for days, even weeks at a time, and eventually, began even to love him. He let her have a cat. He promised to send her to school. She hoped to become a nurse.

I can't even begin to describe what I'm feeling now, the disgust about Roger's scheme, the horror and pain of losing Mary, the wrenching feeling that I somehow led her to death. Why hadn't I paid closer attention to the herbs she'd wanted me to buy? Why hadn't I secured the house? Where did I get the neo-colonialist notion that I should take charge of this Filipina's life, as if my own wretched existence was something to admire and model, as if I could manage her life any better than I'd managed my own? I have

now been awake for twenty-six hours and I'm starting to hallucinate flies on the wall.

'Til next time,

V

March 17

Reverend Lee just left. I called him last night, woke
up his wife (who seemed irritated). He slept on the
couch in the family room. He brought Pete to school
this morning. He comforted and counseled me, prepared tea for me, held me, prayed with me and
prayed for me until I was finally able to fall asleep. I
told him everything about Roger, Mary, my father,
the unedited version. And through it all, he never
judged, or blamed, or shamed. He listened with an
open heart, and when I was done, he held my hand
and helped me pray. What did I pray for? The power
to face another day, to be the kind of mother my son
deserves, to honor Mary without blaming myself.
And I prayed for the strength to face new challenges:
coming to terms with my father's dying, surviving
the divorce proceedings, and starting a new life as a
woman alone.

Reverend Lee wanted me to pray for the power to
forigve Roger, but I'm not there yet.

'Til next time,

V

March 25

Lynette called at 7 A.M. to remind me about the *Heirloom Roadshow*. "We should probably get there no later than nine if we want to get out stuff appraised."

My eyes were still crusted shut. I didn't think I could wrench myself from bed, but Lynette would not relent. "Come on, Val, you need to get out. Curtis will watch the boys. Besides, you wanted to get that sculpture appraised, didn't you?"

I roused Pete, slapped a cold Pop-Tart on the table, and put new makeup over my old makeup.

As I'd expected, the armory was packed and hot and smelly. There were four video cameras trained on four appraisal tables. Lynette and I chose the table with the shortest line, presided over by a big-boned silver-haired woman who identified herself as Sally. She wore a bright red linen blazer, a long black twill skirt, and those beige leather orthopedic shoes the manufacturers of which try to pass off (unsuccessfully) as sneakers. An hour and five minutes later, it was Lynette's turn. She put her box of plates on the table. Sally quickly examined them, pushed her glasses farther up on her nose, and thumbed through a small reference book. She gestured toward the camera, and it glided toward her. "Lynette, you told me that this china was a gift from your grandmother, yes?"

"Yes, it was a gift from my mother's mother," Lynette answered. "It was a wedding present."

"Do you know where your grandmother obtained it?"

"Um, I think it was her mother's." Lynette's voice was high and gurgly, like a contestant's on *Let's Make a Deal*. I think she sensed, as I did, that her granny's old plates might be worth something.

"Well, Lynette, your grandmother's wedding present is a very fine example of Flow Blue dinnerware. Flow Blue started production in the early 1800s and remained popular for about a hundred years. It's believed that this style was invented by Josiah Wedgewood. Lynette, you've heard of Wedgewood china?"

Lynette shook her head excitedly. "Yes, oh yes!" Lynette turned around and threw me a wild-eyed look.

"Well, Lynette, you may be interested to know that Flow Blue china was produced with a technique known as transfer printing," Sally droned on, in a flat but authoritative voice. "The ink was forced to bleed through the china when a volatizing agent was added, usually ammonia. Early Victorian Flow Blue, which is what you've got here, Lynette, was the first style produced by the company. Lynette, based on the oriental pattern, I believe that this set was produced between 1835 and 1850. Lynette, do you want to know what your grandmother's dinnerware is worth?"

"Yes, oh yes!"

"Lynette, your grandmother's Flow Blue dinnerware has an estimated value of $200,000."

Lynette jumped to her feet and clutched at her chest. "Oh my gosh! Oh my gosh!" She waved her hands in front of her face to stave off tears of joy. "Thank you so much!"

"You are most welcome, Lynette," the woman said, signaling for me to sit down. "Your name?" she asked.

I cleared my throat. "Valerie Ryan." I tried to angle my head so I wouldn't appear to have more than a single chin.

"Okay, Valerie, let's see what you've brought us today." The camera moved in as I pulled the piece out of my canvas tote bag. Sally bent forward and pushed her glasses back up. "Tell me about this piece, Valerie."

"Well, this was given to me for my birthday. It's bronze and I have been told it was in the family for a while. I think it originally belonged to Franklin and Eleanor Roosevelt, a gift from the queen of England."

The woman turned the piece in her hands, ran her index finger over it. I felt light-headed. I couldn't wait to cash in.

"Well, Valerie, this is an interesting piece indeed," she began. "It was a gift, you say?"

"Yes, a gift from, uh . . . it was a gift."

Sally looked at me over the top of her glasses.

"Well, Valerie, have you heard of Frederic Remington?"

I nodded slowly. Oh my God, Roger had given me a Remington?

"Valerie, Frederic Remington was born in 1861 in Canton, New York," Sally began in her flat way. "Remington's illustrations, paintings, and bronze castings captured the wild adventure of the American frontier. Valerie, your little cowboy here is an example of the Remington style. I believe it was produced sometime around 1975."

I assumed she meant to say 1875. I didn't interrupt her.

"If this sculpture had been bronze, it would be worth perhaps a thousand dollars, maybe more. Your piece, however, is painted plaster, Valerie, and actually a very nice example of painted plaster at that. Because your piece is in decent condition, Valerie, I would place its value at about thirty-five dollars."

"I'm sorry? Thirty-five dollars?"

The woman turned to the cameraman and gestured for him to cut. "Valerie, your piece is what we in the business call a WPOC."

"Excuse me?"

"A Worthless Piece of Crap, Valerie." She scratched a small spot on the back with her fingernail, exposing the white plaster beneath. "I'm sorry, Valerie." On line behind me, a burly old man in red plaid shorts snickered. Everyone else pretended they hadn't heard Sally's appraisal.

I stood up. "Thank you, Sally." I grabbed my plaster cowboy off the table and chucked it in an empty metal trash bin. I peered inside and was happy to see that his head had cracked off.

'Til next time,

V

March 26

I'm finally starting to feel like myself again. I found the strength to clean the house, and it felt good to pack up the rest of Roger's things. I was aware that I felt no longing, no sadness, not the slightest wistfulness. Just a gratifying sense of completion as I rolled the strapping tape across the boxes and marked them with a black Sharpie: R. Tisdale. Right then I was glad that I hadn't changed my name to his.

'Til next time,

V

March 27

Spent the morning with Omar Sweet. According to the laws in our state, Roger is guilty of third degree "criminal sexual conduct" if he engaged in penetration with someone under sixteen. But Mary obviously can't testify, and it would be hard to prove they had sex unless there was a witness. Since it's unlikely that Roger sold tickets to the deflowering of his virgin "bride," it looks like I'm the one who's screwed now.

'Til next time,
V

March 29

I had a nightmare about Roger. I dreamed that he was sitting on the edge of the bed, holding out a red rose. When I reached out to take it from him, the flower turned into a crow. It snapped its sharp beak down on my fingers and wouldn't let go, and the pain was unbearable. I tried to shake it off, but it wouldn't release me. I woke up sweating and crying, and couldn't get back to sleep until four in the morning. I really feel and look like crap now but I've got to get myself together for Pete's school carnival. I have been assigned to staff something called the "toilet toss." I have no idea what that is, but given my appearance and general state of mind, it seems appropriate.

'Til next time,
V

March 30

The toilet toss involves a real porcelain toilet and a bucket of beanbags. The toilet was provided by a Mushroomhead whose husband owns a plumbing company. I'm trying not to make any paranoid assumptions about how I was chosen to staff that particular game.

'Til next time,

V

April 1

As Pete and I drove to the mall, a police car came screaming up behind me. I was sure it was after me (busted brake light) but when I pulled the Jeep over, the car sped past me and pulled into the Arby's parking lot. Close behind, two firetrucks and a second police car.

As we passed, I saw an elderly man on the sidewalk, facedown and motionless. The two ambulance drivers knelt beside him. "What's going on, Mom?" Pete asked.

"I don't know, honey." I reached back and squeezed his hand. "I don't know."

Pete was quiet for a long time. Finally, he asked me, "What is death, Mommy?"

Oh boy. I wasn't ready for this conversation.

"Well, nobody really knows, sweetheart," I began. I talked about the concept of the spirit, the soul. I briefly described how death was viewed in other cultures and civilizations, like the Egyptians. I talked about heaven, rebirth, the circle of life. I reminded him about his goldfish, and the parakeet. "Even though we don't know for sure what it's like to be dead, sweetie, a lot of people are pretty sure that it's not an ending, but a kind of beginning, of a new kind of life." I was rather proud of my response to Pete's question, considering I hadn't even prepared.

I watched Pete's expression through the rearview mirror. He looked confused. "What is it, sweetie?"

"I thought it's when you can't hear. Hunter says his great uncle Harry is deaf. He talks with his hands."

"Deaf? I thought you asked me what it's like to be dead."

"I already know all about that," he said, rolling his eyes. "It's when your heart stops. Can you put on my Frog and Toad tape, please?"

'Til next time,

V

April 2

If I'd ever wondered what Ben Murphy has been up to, or whether he might make a suitable mate, I have my answer.

I brought Pete downtown to see a local group called the Marvelous Merlin Society perform outside the public library. (Pete's been interesting in King Arthur ever since we rented a video called *A Kid in King Arthur's Court*.) I'd seen the group around town before, a motley crew that could euphemistically be described as artistic, but realistically as geeky losers. On May Day they skip through the streets shaking tambourines festooned with crepe paper streamers. There's a juggler who uses only two beanbags. Even I can juggle two beanbags.

The show began with a miming court jester who clambered around like a monkey in an attempt to engage the audience. He danced around a toddler, who started screaming. His mother carried him away. Then he swiped at a woman's lovely and quite expensive straw hat (I recognized it from the Talbot's window), sending it flying into the street, where it was promptly flattened by a teenage girl on a dirty yellow moped. The menacing mime/jester finally took his leave, and then the musicians appeared, playing bells, small stringed instruments, and wooden flutes.

Then I saw Ben. He was dressed in orange tights, a billowy white blouse, and big green bloomers with velvet suspenders. He wore pointy black satin slippers and a garland of shriveled yellow dandelions on his head. He was dancing a kind of hopping jig, arms linked with a fair maiden who was actually quite agile for someone her size.

After a few lively turns, Ben and his lady started dancing in my direction. He didn't seem to notice me. I ducked my head into my bag and kept it there for the rest of the performance. I would have left if it hadn't been for Pete, who thoroughly enjoyed the show and, when it was all done, asked if he could meet the jester. I told him we had to move the Jeep or we'd get a ticket, and I was glad he was young enough to think meter maids work on weekends.

I guess Ben Murphy wasn't really right for me in the first place.

'Til next time,

V

April 5

A local woman is missing.

The story was on page two of today's paper, an odd position considering that no one ever disappears in this town, unless some camper gets sloshed and passes out in the woods. The second page is usually reserved for obituaries, car accidents, DWIs and the occasional lost farm animal (last summer it was a fugitive ostrich). And it's an odd position considering the stories that made it to page one: Chung Foo restaurant closes. Seventy-three-year-old grandmother earns high school diploma. City council approves north side shopping center. Public pools open for business.

And there on page two, the story of a thirty-eight-year-old woman who never returned home after her morning run around Machick Park on Monday morning. When she hadn't shown up for work, her boss called her at home. Her roommate was worried too. Zoe Hayes apparently was conscientious to the point of fussiness. Her weekday morning schedule never varied: She ran from 6:30 to 7:40, returned home to shower and change for work, arrived at her desk at the hospital radiography department by 8:30. "It's not like her to just disappear," the roommate was quoted as saying. "I don't understand it."

There was a photograph too. Dark hair pulled back into a tight ponytail, dark, wide-set eyes, a small mouth parted to reveal a row of square white teeth. Her smile seemed guarded or forced, as if to placate a cajoling photographer.

'Til next time,

𝒱

April 6

Zoe Hayes made it to page one. Headline: Police suspect foul play. Her father, a retired lieutenant, has flown in from New Mexico. There are search parties now, friends, neighbors, hospital co-workers; members of her running club are retracing all her routes—the park, around Kimball Lake, out by the county airport, over by the Caswell farm. They're putting up fliers, sending out chain e-mail (I got one today and promptly sent it to everyone on my distribution list who lives in town). There was a prayer vigil last night at the park.

I don't know this woman, yet I can't seem to stop thinking about her.

I also haven't stopped thinking of Roger. It kills me to think that he might get away with everything he's done, just because I didn't have a witness to his relationship with Mary.

'Til next time,

𝒱

April 6, continued

Feeling utterly invisible and worthless is actually a good thing, now and then, isn't it? A kind of Buddhist exercise in humility, yes? At least that's what I've tried to convince myself after today's experience in Pete's class.

Since Pete's birthday falls during the spring, he celebrates with other kids who also have spring birthdays. This year I baked four million chocolate chip blondies and fudge brownies and mixed several jugs of pink lemonade. I packed it up in a plastic milk carton and toted it to his classroom, feeling pleased that I had performed at least one maternal feat with a degree of competence.

Two other mothers of spring-birthday kids were also there, and they were Mushroomheads, the ones who raise money for the art museum every year, and not because they believe it's a worthy cause, but because this annual fund-raising campaign has become a social event that carries as much cachet as country club membership and provides a good excuse to buy a new gown.

As the Shitakes chattered away by the aquarium, I bent down to offer a tray of brownies. "Ladies?" I said, in my friendliest tone, hating them completely. One glanced over in the direction of the tray, but said nothing. The other one never looked up, and never stopped talking ("So I *told* him, if you can't match the *tile* to the *trim*, just *forget* it."). I stood there stupidly, not sure if I should offer the brownies again, or walk away. I stood there. And then I walked away.

A police dog found a dirty white Footlocker crew sock, which may or may not belong to Zoe Hayes.

'Til next time,

𝒱

April 7

Bad news: The sock belongs to Zoe Hayes.

Her father has announced a $100,000 reward for "information leading to the arrest and conviction of the person or persons responsible" for his daughter's disappearance. The police department is now working with the FBI, a collaboration that seems promising—if our local cops can't figure this out, surely the FBI will. This morning's paper mentioned that there are some similarities between this case and a series of murders in New York. The Long Island Kennel Killer. Some nut kept women in a dog cage. I don't even want to think about it.

'Til next time,

V

April 8

No new clues, but plenty of rumors. The most disturbing theory I've heard is that she was left for dead in a Dumpster, and now she's on life support at the hospital. There are morbid variations on this theme. I overheard Hunter tell Pete that the "lost lady is being kept alive in the hospital but she doesn't have a head." I could see the horrified look in Pete's eyes; I told him it was a crazy rumor, but the truth is it gave me the creeps, and still does.

In moments like these I remember how secure it felt to have another grown-up in the house. Maybe *secure* is the wrong word. Maybe *grown-up* is the wrong word too. But I'd be lying if I said I feel just as safe in this house without Roger. He was the designated investigator of all noises in the night. He kept a crowbar under his side of the bed, and he'd grab it if he heard anything suspicious. Now I'm the noise investigator by default and I don't sleep as deeply anymore. I'm not even sure I'm sleeping at all. I feel like I'm just wading in that shallow zone where it's hard to know the difference between thoughts and dreams. When the alarm clock sounds I don't feel rested, just drained. I've tried to write down these dreams, but I can't conjure the details.

Omar managed to have Roger arrested on bigamy charges. His parents promptly bailed him out. Roger's hearing isn't for another two weeks. It is unlikely that he'll serve any time in jail.

My mother wants me to tell Pete that his father has been arrested. "Just tell him he's a bad man who did a bad thing," she told me on the phone this morning. She thinks I should do everything possible to sever the ties between them, and in doing so, cut Roger out of my life forever, "like the malignant tumor that he is." The words just hung there.

We try to be careful in conversation now, but the

more self-conscious we are, the more we stumble into these conversational pitfalls. Last week, for instance, Mom was listing all these women she knew who had gotten boob jobs, and I asked her if she'd consider having one herself. "Are you kidding?" she laughed. "Your father would die!" Then she quickly added, "I mean, he'd go bananas."

Mom likes to think she's not superstitious, but we both know that's a lie. Whenever she reports that Dad's having a good day, she immediately searches for some wood surface to knock on, even if it means going into another room. Last week she put fresh batteries in the cuckoo clock, the one she gave my father for his fiftieth birthday. I suspect she believes that as long as the clock still ticks, so will Dad.

I understand these superstitions. Ever since my father was diagnosed with prostate cancer, I always drop coins in every charity canister, whether the cause is cancer research or a new kidney for the kid who's waiting for a transplant. Of course, I know that there is no causal relationship between Dad's prognosis and my donations. I can't help myself.

'Til next time,

cv

April 11

The Zoe Hayes story seems to be receding from the headlines. It's still worthy of front-page news, but the column space shrinks a little more as each day passes with no new leads. Now it's at the bottom of the page, no photo. The search parties are done searching. The FBI investigators have packed up and gone home.

The one question the paper hasn't raised is this: If Zoe Hayes had been abducted, doesn't that mean there may be a kidnapper somewhere in our town? And if she was murdered, is there a murderer among us?

'Til next time,

V

April 13

I had a dream about Zoe Hayes. I wasn't in the dream, exactly, but floating somewhere above everything, just watching. Zoe was in a bird cage, the kind they sell at Pier 1 for decorative use only because any normal bird would peck his way out in a jiffy. The cage was swinging back and forth and she was hopping from one perch to the next, like a canary. She smiled as she hopped to the highest level, which looked like one of those little plastic bird swings. In a heap at the bottom of the cage were the kind of clothes I thought she might have worn for her job at the hospital: a white lab coat, a pair of white soft-soled shoes, and a clipboard with an X ray attached to it. I was able to get a closer look at the X ray. It was of a bird's wing. I understood that the wing had been broken, but somehow I could also tell that it was on the mend. At the bottom of the X ray, in sparkling red letters, was the word ABILENE.

I woke up at 3 A.M. gasping for air, trying to make sense of this crazy dream. Had someone captured Zoe in a cage? Did he break her arms? Had he stripped off her lab coat? Was she smiling because she was dead, and in a better place now?

In today's paper, as police seem less hopeful about turning up new clues, Zoe's father renewed his appeal for leads. "If anyone out there knows anything about my daughter, I want to hear from you," he's quoted as saying. "Even if it's just a half-baked theory, I want to hear it. I refuse to give up hope." I think I'll call him.

'Til next time,

V

April 14

When I woke up this morning I changed my mind. Zoe Hayes's father must have had enough crackpot calls and dead-end leads. But when I told my mother about the dream, she urged me to make the call. Then she told me something I'd never known, that when I was a little girl, she and Dad had speculated that I might be psychic.

"You're kidding."

"No, I'm quite serious, Valerie. You were about three, maybe four years old. You woke up from a nap and announced, 'Poppy's Impala is going to break today.' Clear as a bell. I remember it like it was yesterday. You were wearing your red corduroy overalls and a red and white striped shirt with the matching red and white striped socks. And sure enough, your grandfather's car died that day."

I told my mother I thought that hardly qualified as an ESP dream, especially if my grandfather's car was some old clunker.

"No, that's the point. The Impala was brand new! It still had the dealer sticker on the window. We thought your dream was hilarious. But nobody was laughing when Poppy broke down on I-75, believe me." She paused. "And there was another time."

"Tell me."

"You were six. You and your sisters had just come home from school and you were having a snack in the kitchen. Chocolate ice cream and chocolate-covered graham crackers, as I recall." (It figures.) "I was reading the newspaper and I guess you were sort of looking at the paper over my shoulder. There was a photo of Margaret Rollins, the lady who ran White Mountain Nursery and Landscaping over in Uniondale. There was a little blurb about Margaret's presentation to the garden club."

"And?"

"And you pointed at her picture and said, 'That lady is dead.' I looked at you and told you that I'd been at the garden club presentation myself and Margaret Rollins was most certainly alive. But you were adamant about it. You just kept saying, 'No, Mother, that lady is dead.' And wouldn't you know, the next day there's a picture of Margaret Rollins in the obituaries. Died of a heart attack in the K-Mart parking lot. Forty-six years old. I calculated that she must have been dead about twenty minutes when you announced it there in the kitchen."

Goosebumps prickled my arms. "How come you never told me any of this?"

"Well, we didn't want to make a big deal about it. We did mention the whole thing to Reverend Kinkaid—you remember him?"

"Vaguely." I remember that he looked like a big white potato, and he needed a bra.

"A good man, but a little too extreme for my taste. As far as he was concerned, we were all going to hell in a handbasket." Mom sighed. "Anyway, we told him about your dreams and he got pretty worked up over it. He said that only God could foretell the future and we should forget the whole thing, otherwise we were just tempting the devil."

"Did you really believe that?"

"Not at all. But we didn't want you to grow up thinking you were weird. So we didn't exactly cultivate your ESP—assuming that's what those incidents were and not just a couple of coincidences. We just let it go. And as far as we knew, the vision about Margaret Rollins was the last of it."

"Until now," I said.

"Yes."

"Or maybe not," I said. "Maybe it was just a plain old dream."

"Maybe. But I still think you ought to call, Val. When I think of what that poor man must be going through, a living nightmare. I'll tell you, it makes you want to count your blessings."

I got off the phone and logged onto the computer to check out the website, findzoe.com. I sent this e-mail:

"I am so sorry about your daughter's disappearance. For what it's worth, I dreamed that your daughter was in a little bird cage, and she was hopping from one perch to the next." I went on to describe my dream in greater detail, and the more I wrote, the more ridiculous my dream seemed to me. "I should tell you," I concluded, "that I don't consider myself a psychic, but I recently learned that I may have had a couple of ESP experiences when I was a little girl, according to my mother. It was her idea to contact you about my dream. I hope you find your daughter soon, and I pray that she is alive and well. If you need more information, feel free to e-mail me at vryan61@hotmail.com."

I held my breath as I hit the send button. Until

that point, I was just another spectator, one of thousands in our town who read about Zoe Hayes in the paper and empathized with her family—at a distance. But with that click of the mouse, I was now involved in the drama. My dream is now part of the Zoe Hayes story, even if it doesn't amount to anything, even if her father never calls me. Now I feel connected to Zoe Hayes in a way I hadn't felt before.

I'm not sure I like this feeling.

Checked my e-mail. Got a response from findzoe. com acknowledging receipt of my message. It was basically a form letter. I guess no one is taking my dream too seriously. I'm actually relieved.

'Til next time,

V

April 17

In the absence of any other witnesses or evidence, it's unlikely that Roger will be convicted of statutory rape, let alone bigamy. Omar said he knows Roger's lawyer—supposedly the best criminal defense attorney in the Midwest.

On the other hand, Omar says that we can expect the divorce to go smoothly, and he can almost guarantee full custody of Pete and a generous settlement—all Roger's hidden assets plus the house and half of all holdings he reported in the deposition. I'm happy about all that, but it would absolutely kill me if Roger walked away from this mess without serving time.

'Til next time,

V

April 19

I heard the phone ring as I was pulling into the garage and I raced to grab it. I was panting when I snatched up the receiver. I should have checked Caller ID first.

"Hi, baby. Awww, you're all out of breath. I hope I'm not interrupting anything." There was a low chuckle.

"What do you want, Eddie?"

"Hey, what's wrong? I thought you'd be at least a little happy to hear from me."

"You thought wrong, Eddie. You weren't exactly gentle that day in your truck, or the time before that in my house."

"How do you figure?" He laughed. "If *my* memory serves, you always liked it a little rough. 'I *love* being swept away. I *love* being overpowered,' 'I *love* a man who takes charge,'" he mimicked in a falsetto. "Those were your words, sweetheart, not mine."

My head throbbed. He wasn't wrong. I'd made the confession in one of those self-revelatory conversations characteristic of new lust. I was a little drunk and extremely horny. "For the record, I was not turned on."

There was a long silence. "I'm sorry," he said finally. "I'd never do anything to hurt you. I love you, Val."

"Okay, Eddie," I said, gliding over the l-word. "Look, I really should go. I've got ice cream melting on the counter."

"No! Wait! I need to talk to you. Listen. Me and Patty, we're separated."

"Again?" I sighed.

"This time it's for real. And I know it's the right thing. It was my decision to move out. But . . . I don't know. I just need to talk to you."

"I don't think that's a good idea, Eddie."

"Oh, come on. Please. I just want to see you. I swear I won't touch you."

I agreed to see him. I told him I'd stop by tomorrow on my way back from the club. Yes, I know I'm an idiot.

'Til next time,

V

April 20

Pete woke up with the flu, too hot and miserable to go to school. I scrolled back my Caller ID until I found Eddie's new number. I expected his husky voice, but got one of those automated, monotone recordings: Please leave message. I mention's Pete's flu and said we'd have to reschedule.

Pete has a fever of 102° and he's in an awful mood, but he refuses to take medicine. I've tried cherry-flavored, grape-flavored, bubble-gum-flavored. Liquid, chewables, the kind that dissolves instantly like cotton candy. I begged, bribed, and coaxed. When that didn't work, I tried browbeating him into submission and said some things I regret ("If you don't take this you'll wind up in the hospital where they're going to give you a shot!"), but he just clamped his lips shut and turned away. I sometimes wonder whether Pete is a latent Christian Scientist. His aversion to medicine is like some deeply held conviction. He won't even let me put a cool washcloth on his forehead. I have fantasies of strapping him to the bed and shoving the spoonful of medicine down his throat. I was sorry to have to keep him home today—his class was going on a little field trip to a fire station. I'd bought him the wooden Mancala set he coveted after playing the game for the first time at Hunter's birthday party. I wanted to give it to him this afternoon, but I could tell he was in no shape to play, so I tucked it under his bed.

God, I *hate* it when my kid gets sick! I'm always leaping to the most catastrophic possibility when there's no reason to think it's anything other than an ordinary virus.

Pete has been asleep for four hours. It's almost dinnertime. I'm going to go wake him up. . . .

I'm back. Pete's still sleeping. This is sad: When I went in to wake him, he shakily raised himself up on one elbow and blinked at me. His face was flushed and his eyes were glassy. I knew he was still sleeping. He looked right through me. "Daddy? You're home?"

"No, sweetie, it's Mommy. You're sleeping. You're dreaming."

He beamed joyfully and (still sleeping) said, "Oh, Daddy, I'm so glad you're back. I knew you'd come back." He flopped onto the pillow and murmured something I couldn't quite make out, then started working his mouth as if he were nursing. I called my mother, the one person I knew would bolster my decision to cut Roger (aka "the tumor") out of my life. Unfortunately, she was in the middle of giving Dad his four million pills and couldn't talk.

I've decided to let Pete sleep through dinner. When he wakes up, I'll see if he's in any mood to talk about his father. Interesting: Pete never brings up Roger when he's awake, but only when he's asleep—delirious, even. Similarly, Roger was most intimate when he was talking in his sleep. In this urgent voice he'd say things like, "You're a wonderful woman." Or, "I don't know what I'd do without you." Or, "I really do love you." Of course, he might have been addressing one of a thousand conquests, but somehow I always believed he was talking to me, saying things he didn't have the inclination or courage to say during wakefulness.

'Til next time,
V

April 21

My printer is broken, Pete is still sick and he still won't take any medicine. He slept most of the day while I paid bills and balanced the checkbook. I have exactly $7,947 in checking. My average monthly expenses are:

$1560 mortgage (thank God we refinanced last year)

$125 electric

$75 gas

$60 water (why is it so damn high? Is there a toilet running somewhere in this house? Must call water company to check.)

$190 phone

$35 cell phone

$28 basic cable service

$275 Jeep payment (he refused to buy the cars with cash, even though he could well afford to)

$255 van payment (yes, I continue to pay off Roger's van because the title is in my name, something I stupidly agreed to years ago)

$129 home equity loan

$450 groceries

$140 gas (it cost me $35 to fill up yesterday. Jeez!)

$12 local paper

$35 *Chicago Tribune*

$40 lawnmowing service (May through September)

This doesn't include Pete's camp fees, new clothes and shoes for Pete, life and health insurance, homeowner's and auto insurance, dry cleaning (gotta try Dryel), eating out, birthday presents, car wash, cosmetics, medical visits. Add it all up, and I have enough money in checking for about two more months of bills.

Why the hell didn't I put some money aside and invest in the stock market? I feel like such a loser, like there was a big money festival going on and everyone went except me. Some of my neighbors are now multimillionaires, all because they bought some hot technology stocks and cashed in at the right time. There are now rows of shiny new Lexuses and Lincoln Navigators and BMWs parked in driveways that were occupied by Ford Tauruses and Toyota Camrys only a couple of years ago.

My parents always said the stock market was just

another slot machine. They didn't play either, and now my mother barely has enough money to cover Dad's medical bills. This divorce settlement had better happen fast—and it had better be generous—or I'm going to have to find a job. Which wouldn't be the worst thing in the world, but I'd rather not have to work until Pete goes back to school in the fall.

'Til next time,
𝒱

April 22

Pete is up and around but he's still running a fever, so we're homebound again today. Kevin was nice enough to stop by and pick up the broken printer. I asked him to stay for coffee and we finished off half a tray of butterscotch brownies. Kevin stood up and stretched like a little boy. His T-shirt inched up to reveal a flat belly, a few wispy blond hairs. "Can you direct me to your bathroom?"

"Sure. First door on your right." I started clearing the plates.

Pete appeared in the foyer. "What's that noise, Mommy?"

I didn't hear anything.

Pete pointed toward the bathroom door. "Listen."

Actually, I *did* hear a faint buzz coming from the general vicinity of the bathroom. I figured it was the toilet or maybe the air-conditioning. But when Kevin opened the bathroom door and saw us both standing there, he seemed flustered.

"Oh, hi, this is my son, Peter," I said, hoping to break the tension.

Kevin wiped his damp hand on his shorts then stuck it out. "Much obliged," he said, smiling. He knelt down. "I'm going to fix your mom's copy machine. Do you like fixing stuff?

Pete nodded happily. "I fixed my bike when the wheel got stuck. And I took apart my radio and put it back together."

"Really? That's amazing. I took apart a Game Boy the other day." It didn't seem like Kevin was doing this to impress me. He seemed genuinely engaged. He told me later that he loves kids, especially when they're still unselfconsiously curious about the world. When Kevin needs what he calls a "kid fix," he visits his sister in Detroit. "She and my brother-in-law have two boys and a girl and they think I'm the coolest guy in the world because I know who Pikachu is."

"Hey, I know who Pikachu is! He's that yellow Pokémon with the lightning bolt tail."

Kevin grinned and tapped me on the nose. "Then I guess that makes you the coolest girl in the world."

"I guess so."

I called Eddie, told him I wanted to reschedule for Friday, when I was sure Pete would be back on his feet. Eddie offered to come by the house, but I quickly told him that would be a bad idea. After I hung up the phone I closed all the shades and locked all the doors and windows.

I checked my e-mail again. Word of my divorce must have finally hit the Center, because I'm suddenly getting mail from the social workers and secretaries. Everyone wants to know how I'm holding up (fine, I lied), and they're worried about Pete. Seeing the Center's address and phone number at the bottom of the e-mails reminded me of my old boss Cadence and the hideous spectacle I made of myself—not once, but on countless occasions, in meetings, in her office, even at the awards ceremony, where I managed to attach a tablecloth to my waistband and drag away the entire table setting, centerpiece and all. I find myself masochistically imagining Cadence's smug reaction to the news that my marriage—my whole life, in fact—has blown apart. In my worst nightmare, I am groveling at Cadence's feet, begging for a job, any job. She gives me a gofer job, and I spend my workdays running her personal errands. I see myself squatting behind her Rottweilers to scoop up their droppings.

No e-mail messages from Zoe Hayes's father. I guess he doesn't consider my dream a hot lead. Fine. I'm glad I sent the e-mail, because if Zoe *had* turned up in a little bird cage somewhere, I would have felt unspeakably remorseful keeping my dream to myself.

The search effort has all but fizzled out. The first couple of weeks were filled with energy and hope as fliers were posted and search parties with police dogs scoured the area. Now the yellow ribbons they wrapped around trees and fence posts are ragged, and the newspaper has no coverage, not even a line or two. To date, the only trace of the missing woman is a single crew sock. There are fewer female runners on the roads and in the park now, and more men than women are walking the family dogs after dark.

'Til next time,

V

April 23

Pete is still home and bored out of his mind, but I'm tired of playing entertainment director. Such is the plight of my only child. He's just not skilled at occupying himself and my patience usually expires after the seventh hand of old maid (which I've been compelled by political correctness to rename "big loser"). In a couple of weeks he goes to camp, and we're both thrilled! I think I may be ready to go back to work.

'Til next time,

V

April 26

It's soggy and drizzling and I have a headache. I want to put together a résumé but what's the point if I have no printer? Or am I just procrastinating?

I called Eddie to confirm our appointment. I suggested we meet at the public library (*public* being the operative word), but Eddie insisted he didn't feel well enough to go out and said he'd feel more comfortable talking privately. I'm meeting him at his apartment.

'Til next time,

V

April 27

I dragged myself out of bed this morning and studied myself in the mirror. My eyes were smeared with yesterday's mascara and my hair was as dull as dirty laundry. I wore one of Roger's discarded Nike T-shirts and a pair of black Victoria's Secret panties that fit rather nicely—two years ago, for about twenty minutes; now the elastic waistband cuts into my belly and leaves jagged red marks. My upper arms and inner thighs jiggle gelatinously and I could successfully hide a crack pipe in my chin.

I know I've gained some weight since last summer, but don't know for sure how much, since I refuse to weigh myself. Besides, all I really need to do to confirm my expanding girth is simply look at the tag in my pants. I'm up one size now and growing. Why is it that I'm either losing weight or gaining, but never just holding steady? My doctor had said I might gain weight on Prozac, but I hadn't expected it to happen so quickly. I knew I was getting fat, but it hadn't bothered me much, though I suppose that's probably another effect of the drug.

But today I'd wanted to be lean and pretty, not hideously bloated. Today I would meet Eddie, and while I had no interest in sleeping with him, I felt compelled to look attractive, relatively speaking. This has nothing to do with Eddie, and everything to do with growing up in a house where makeup was as essential as shoes. You didn't leave the house without it. I remember the first words from my sister's mouth not six hours after I'd delivered Pete. I was in my hospital bed, still heady with joy and drugs. Teresa walked in and said, "Put on some lipstick, would you? You look like death!" My mother nodded in agreement and began searching her bag, smiling as she pulled a gleaming gold tube from its depths. "Have lipstick, will travel!" she said cheerily, and tossed the tube onto my lap.

I yanked open the bathroom drawer in search of something that might transform me. I found the Preparation-H (bought it after I read that it's great for firming your face. Brings new meaning to the term "butthead." Never had the nerve to try it); six May-belline lip crayons purchased purely on impulse at the supermarket; wet eye pads that look and smell exactly like raw cucumber slices; twelve different foundations, ranging from porcelain to medium beige (none of which matches my skin tone, which, on this day, could be most accurately described as piss yellow); a little pot of coconut-scented body glitter (bought at Claire's in a moment of self-delusion). I slammed the drawer shut and climbed into the shower.

Despite the heat, I chose a black top with three-quarter-length sleeves to hide my upper arms, and pulled on my only nice pants, black Tencel with a flat front and side zipper. I pulled my hair back, slapped on some Origins Pinch Your Cheeks and lipstick, and rammed a Pop-Tart into my mouth, then washed it down with a can of diet Coke.

I dropped Pete and Hunter off at school, silently cursed all the skinny young mothers with their flat bellies and long legs, then headed west. As I drove downtown, I ran through all the possible and improbable reasons for Eddie's sudden desire to see me:

1. He's madly in love with me and can't live without me.

2. He wants to have sex.

3. He needs money.

4. He's moving to Idaho to join a militia, and wants to bid me farewell.

5. He's considering starting psychotherapy and wants a referral.

6. He's taking art lessons and wants to draw me. Naked.

7. He's gay.

8. All of the above.

9. None of the above.

I stared at the green steel door and suddenly felt the impulse to turn around and run back to the Jeep. I can't explain it exactly. I wouldn't say it was a guardian angel, or some supernatural voice urging me to run. I just felt I should leave. Fast.

I started to turn when the door suddenly swung open and Eddie pulled me inside. He hugged me. I stiffened against him. "I'm so glad you came," he whispered. He closed the door behind me and locked it, first the deadbolt, then a rusty chain. "I'm so glad you came," he repeated, and I saw that his eyes were watery, as if he might cry.

The small apartment was hot and airless. The blinds in the living room were drawn closed. The room was sparsely furnished. I recognized a few pieces from his office, the yellow leather couch and a coffee table strewn with empty Fritos bags and candy wrappers. A small TV was on the floor in the corner. *Wheel of Fortune.* No sound.

Eddie gestured toward the couch, but I didn't want to sit down. I didn't want to do anything that might lead him to believe I planned to stay for more than a few minutes.

"You know I hate to drink alone, but I guess I'll make an exception in this case." He sauntered toward the galley kitchen and disappeared behind a wall. "I think I'll put in a Tombstone pizza. Pepperoni okay?"

"Fine," I called out, wondering how I'd eat when I had no appetite. I felt my stomach clench, followed by an urgent need to use the toilet. I hunted in my purse for Immodium but found only a couple of loose Tic-Tacs. There were two doors, both closed. I guessed that one was the bathroom, the other a bedroom. I moved toward the first door and turned the knob. It was locked. My cramps worsened. I turned the other doorknob. The bathroom door opened. I scurried in and locked the door behind me.

I laid some toilet paper down on the seat and lowered myself onto it. I ran the water to mask the sounds of my intestinal distress. I could hear Eddie calling to me from the kitchen. "Val? Val?"

"I'm in the bathroom, Eddie," I yelled out. "Give me a minute."

"You're where?"

"The bathroom," I shouted louder. Soon he was at the other side of the door, rattling the knob.

"I need a minute in here," I said, panicked that he'd try to come in while I was on the toilet. "It's that time of the month," I lied.

But he wasn't giving up. "Let me in," he whispered.

"Please, Eddie, what's gotten into you? I'm not feeling well. I need a little privacy here." I hurried to finish, flushed, and washed my hands.

That's when I noticed it, the hamper, and the little flash of pink peeking out beneath Eddie's dirty underwear and T-shirts. Instinctively I pulled at the fabric.

It was a small nylon jersey.

Frantically, with the water still running and Eddie rattling the doorknob, I dug deeper in the bin.

"I was hoping you wouldn't use the bathroom," Eddie whispered through the door. "I didn't have a chance to clean it."

"That's okay, Eddie, I promise I won't look. Just let me finish up and I'll be right out. Why don't you go check on the pizza?"

"The pizza's fine. Come out."

"You know how it is with women's plumbing. Give me a second." I reached into the hamper up to my elbow and pulled up more clothes, a couple of Eddie's Old Navy T-shirts, jeans, more underwear.

And a pair of black spandex shorts, women's size small. At the very bottom of the hamper, a single crew sock. I held my breath. Could these belong to Zoe Hayes?

I stared into the hamper and I felt the adrenaline scorch my chest. Maybe the clothes belonged to one of Eddie's daughters, I fleetingly considered, or a girlfriend. Or maybe they were his. Each wild theory only escalated my panic. I knew this: the spandex outfit and the single Footlocker crew sock were precisely those items mentioned in every newspaper article, and in every neon green flyer posted on every window and telephone pole in town.

I gulped back the rising knot in my throat. I could hear Eddie tinkering with the doorknob, and right then I believed in my soul that I'd never make it out of the apartment alive. They say your life passes in front of your eyes when you're about to die, but now it wasn't my past, but my future that appeared like a slide show in my head. I saw all the promises I had yet to fulfill, all the milestones and all the ordinary moments of a regular life. I hadn't gone grocery shopping this week. I never organized my front hall closet—how would anyone ever find my will in that mess? Who would make Pete his Charmander chocolate chip pancakes? Who would take him to the Cub Scouts mom-n'-me camp-out? My mind raced further into a forlorn future. I imagined my son learning to drive, filling out his college applications, walking down the aisle, having his first child . . . and I wouldn't be there for any of it. Today was the first time I didn't tell Pete I loved him when we said goodbye. He'd been fiddling with his backpack and I was in a rush to get to Eddie's apartment. The last thing I said when I dropped him off was, "Stop dawdling and get out of the Jeep already." I can't even begin to describe the remorse I felt realizing that those could be my last words to him.

I grabbed my bag and searched for the cell phone, then realized I'd left it plugged into the cigarette lighter in the Jeep. I heard the crisp snap of the lock popping out, and watched as the doorknob twisted. I scrambled to put the clothes back in the hamper, trying to arrange everything as I'd found it. It didn't look right. Was the pink jersey under the briefs or the T-shirts? Jesus. I couldn't remember. The door opened a crack, and I immediately heaved it shut. I heard a wail. "Shit! Shit!" I had shut the door on Eddie's knuckles.

"Oh my God, I'm sorry, Eddie. I didn't mean to . . . I just didn't want you walking in while I was half undressed."

Eddie scanned the room, his eyes lingering on the hamper and then on me. "Why not? It's not like I've never seen your ass before." He nuzzled my neck.

I forced myself to laugh. "Oh, ho! Very true, very true." I sounded like frickin' Angela Lansbury. My right eye started twitching.

Eddie peered at me. "What took you so long?"

"Excuse me?" I answered, feigning indignance. "If you must know, I've got my period and I have cramps. Diarrhea, actually. I'd be happy to describe it for you, if you'd like." I paused and stared at him, clamping down on the insides of my mouth to keep my lips from trembling. "Now, then, aren't you glad you asked?"

I tried to push past Eddie, but he stood there between me and the door. Be cool, be cool, I told myself. My brain kept turning back to the jersey. But I had to behave as if the only thing I'd seen in Eddie's bathroom was the dirty tiles, the only thing I'd touched was the toilet paper. If I bolted for the door, he would know. I had to take my time. And I had to pretend I hadn't noticed the dark look in Eddie's eyes. I had to get out of there. I'd run to my Jeep, and I'd dial 911 from my cell phone. I'd tell them what I'd seen in the bathroom. But first I had to get out of the apartment alive, and I had to make Eddie trust me.

"God, I'm starving. How's that pizza coming along?"

"I thought you had cramps." Eddie stared at me.

"I feel better, thanks," I said, disingenuously interpreting his comment as a sign of concern. "Popped some Advil." I heard myself offer to make a salad but Eddie said he didn't have any lettuce. At this point I pushed toward the doorway and—merciful God—Eddie yielded. "I'm absolutely famished! Let's eat."

When Eddie asked if I was certain I didn't want a beer, I knew my strategy had worked. He seemed happy now, at ease. I was struggling to maintain my equilibrium. The living room seemed smaller, warmer, darker. I had no appetite. Eddie pulled the pizza out of the oven and slapped it directly onto the small table. "You don't have some kind of plate, a cutting board maybe?" I asked, trying to sound casual. I was horrified.

He shrugged sheepishly. "I don't have any of that stuff yet. Mostly I just eat out." He pulled a sharp knife from a drawer and cut long, deep slices across the pie. I heard the blade cut into the Formica, but Eddie didn't seem to notice, or care. Now for the hard part. I lifted the pizza to my mouth and took a bite. My rising panic was intensified by the smell of the cheese. I couldn't eat. I wanted to vomit. Chew the damn pizza, I commanded myself. My teeth moved mechanically. I forced myself to swallow. I felt the pizza move dryly, painfully down my food pipe.

Eddie went back to the kitchen for his third beer.

"So . . . you needed to see me?" I began. "You had something you wanted to tell me?"

Eddie looked at me for a long time. He scraped his fingernails across his stubble, then ran his hands rapidly through his hair as if he was shaking out bugs. He squeezed his eyes shut and dropped his head into his hands. "Things haven't been too good with me, Val. I'm all mixed up."

"What do you mean, mixed up?"

He rubbed his knuckles. "You may not believe this, but you were the best thing that ever happened to me." I couldn't tell where this was leading. I didn't want to say anything that might provoke him, nor did I want to encourage him. I only wanted to escape. I said nothing.

"Maybe I'm nuts, but when you split with Roger, I actually thought we had a chance." He ran a hand over his face and glared at me with bloody red eyes. "Don't you think we would have been good together?"

I nodded slowly, carefully. "Sure, Eddie." Actually, there was a time when I believed it, too. Eddie and I fit together in the way all misfits attract each other; we both suffered through failing marriages, both desperately needed sexual validation. For my part, though, our affair was nothing more than a diversion.

He stared wistfully out the window. "You know, sometimes I wish I could just put you in a little box and throw away the key. I love you so damn much, Val."

I stopped breathing. I tried to smile.

Eddie stood up abruptly. "I gotta pee."

As he sauntered toward the bathroom, I calculated that Eddie's three beers should give me ample time to make it to the front door, and it did. I slid the chain slowly, quietly. But the deadbolt—it was the kind that locked from the inside, with a key. I heard the toilet flush, then almost immediately felt Eddie's warm breath on my neck. "What the hell are you doing?"

I searched for a plausible excuse. "I was checking to make sure the door was locked. I mean, I wouldn't want anyone interrupting us." It was then that I devised my plan.

Finally, Eddie smiled. "Interrupting us doing what?"

"Whatever." I returned the smile. Had I lost my mind? What were my options? I wanted to live. I wanted to see my son again. I didn't want to end up like Zoe Hayes. Did I really believe I could seduce my way out of Eddie's apartment? Actually, I did. I knew that Eddie always fell into a dead sleep after he had an orgasm, especially if he's had a few drinks. I didn't have to have sex, just get him to climax. If I was lucky, I could get away with just using my hand. I'd get the deadbolt key out of his pocket and run like hell.

"Why don't we relax on the couch?" I asked, gesturing toward the leather sofa.

"I've got a better idea." He grinned. "Let's go into the bedroom."

My heart stopped. "The bedroom?"

"Why not?"

Because you've got a dead girl in there, you goddamn lunatic, I wanted to say, but instead heard myself say, "No reason. Bedroom's fine." I watched him pull a plastic drink stirrer out of his back pocket and slip it through the hole in the doorknob. He was sweating now, and breathing heavily. "You'll have to excuse the mess," he said as he opened the door. "I'm working on a project."

"What kind of project?"

Eddie flicked on the light. That's when I saw a sheet draped over what looked to be a big box. Or a cage.

Kate Trager, one of my colleagues at the Center, lived in New York during the "summer of Sam," the summer when David Berkowitz, aka Son of Sam, left his bloody mark on the city. Since the cops had more questions than answers about the elusive killer, every guy on the street seemed like a suspect, especially if you were neurotic, which Kate was. She called the cops a half dozen times with tips on various men—a guy on the subway with an odd-shaped package that might have concealed a gun, a man in a car that lingered a little too long outside the bowling alley. But Kate wasn't alone in her paranoia. Lots of people called in with tips that summer. Everyone was hysterical, desperate. All that summer Kate tucked her long brown hair under her sweatshirt hood no matter how hot the weather, and when she drove in cars, she always crouched under the dashboard, "out of the crosshairs," as she put it.

One afternoon, as Kate was sitting with her mother at the Tip Top diner in Queens, she looked through the window and noticed a man standing by his car in the parking lot. His back was turned, but in that weird telepathic way that exists between strangers, he intuitively knew someone was watching him and slowly swiveled his head around, making direct eye contact with Kate. He smiled and his eyes rolled back in his head. His expression made Kate's skin prickle. She grabbed a pen and jotted down his license number before he drove away. Kate began moving toward the pay phone but her mother dissuaded her. "Enough with this nonsense, already. This is getting ridiculous. Sit down and finish your tuna melt." Kate never did call the cops about the man in the parking lot. But after Son of Sam was captured, and his picture appeared in the *Daily News*, Kate saw that the man in the photograph was the man she had seen that day outside the Tip Top diner.

At the time, his look gave her the creeps, but her real horror came only in retrospect, as she realized how close she had come to making contact with a killer. The stare was an intimacy she never meant to share with him. In all likelihood, Kate was never a target—she was too young, she was in a public place with her mother, it was the middle of the day, and besides, she was wearing her hood. But Kate came away from the experience traumatized, as if she were, in fact, caught in Son of Sam's crosshairs, spared only by some accident of luck.

I got the chills when I first heard that story. But Kate had only brushed shoulders with true evil. I was about to give it a hand job!

Even with the stained sheet draped over the thing

in Eddie's bedroom, I saw enough—the hard squared edges—to know I was looking at some kind of cage, and a big one, too, large enough to confine a St. Bernard or bullmastiff, or, perhaps, a grown woman. My uncle Dennis had used a cage this size for unruly Great Pyrenees while he was at work. The cage was eerily silent and impossible to ignore.

"What's that?" I tried to sound only mildly interested, though I was consumed by the worst imaginings. Is that where he kept her before he killed her? I made myself breathe.

Eddie locked the door behind us. "I told you. A project. Forget about it."

"What kind of project?"

He chuckled softly. "A really fun project." Eddie's face seemed to darken. "Forget about it, okay?" He turned me away from the crate, then gave me a little shove toward the bed. "Take your clothes off."

Call me crazy, but I was determined to get through this ordeal fully dressed. "Mmmmm . . . not so fast, you naughty boy. You first." I ran a finger lightly across his zipper and licked my lips as seductively as I could manage.

Eddie pulled his black T-shirt over his head, exposing his hard belly and hairy chest. "You do the rest," he said, flopping back on the bed, folding his arms behind his head. "Go ahead. Knock yourself out."

I took a deep breath as I unzipped Eddie's jeans.

He wasn't wearing underwear and he was fully aroused. "This is like a dream come true," I heard him mutter. "Honest to God, Val." He lay passively while I struggled to pull his pants off. He grinned happily at me. "Easy, baby, easy. What's the hurry?" I glanced at my wristwatch. 2:19. Pete's school was over in forty minutes. I had to work quickly, efficiently. I tried not to think about the cage. I peeled his pants over his big feet and dropped them on the floor.

"Aren't you going to take your clothes off?"

"No, lover, this is all about you," I forced myself to say. "I want to give you a gift. Just lay back and relax."

"Oh, come on. At least take off your shirt. Give me something to look at."

I undid the top buttons of my blouse, hoping to placate him, but it wasn't enough. He reached over and I held my breath as he unbuttoned the rest and yanked my bra up around my collarbone. "That's better." He fell back on the pillow. "I like a good view." He slogged down another beer, his fourth. Good: The more he drank, the more deeply he would sleep. I also knew that Eddie could be ugly when he was drunk, less rational, more explosive. I had to move quickly.

"Slow down," he muttered. "And use your mouth."

I kept him in my hand; with enough spit and just

the right pressure, he didn't seem to notice the difference. His eyes were rolled back in his head, his hands were clenched, his breathing quickened. Soon. Soon. He was almost there. I went faster, harder. All the while, I mentally reorganized my linen closet, sorting towels by color and size, separating the flat sheets from the fitted . . .

"Keep going," he whispered. "Just like that. Keep . . . it . . . going." With tears in my eyes, I continued working on Eddie until I felt his body stiffen. "There," he whispered. "There. Yes. There. That's it." I wiped my hand along the edge of the mattress. "You're amazing," he muttered, already bleary eyed. "I swear I'll return the favor."

I covered Eddie with the blanket and lay beside him, my head on his chest. "This is the way it should be, the way it was meant to be," he whispered. He absently circled my arm with a fingertip. "We make a helluva team."

I responded with a low "Mmm-hmmm," fearful that anything more articulate might stimulate him to wakefulness. I listened for his breathing to slow and deepen until I was sure he was asleep. He threw a heavy arm across my body, pinning me to the mattress.

I watched Eddie's chest rise and fall. His hands and feet twitched, like a dreaming dog. I could hear the ticking of my wristwatch.

I had to get out of there. I had no idea what was

under that sheet, but I knew with complete certainty that I wanted to pick my son up from school and remain in his life until I died, preferably in my sleep of natural causes at 102 years old. Not now, not here, not by the hand of my former lover.

I snapped my bra back into place and decided to worry about the blouse buttons later. With my heart rioting against my ribs, I slipped my hand into Eddie's jeans, first in the front pockets, then the back. Nothing but a wallet, couple of coins, and the plastic drink stirrer. Jesus. I checked the tiny fifth pocket, but it, too, was empty. Where the hell was that key? I was choking back tears as I scrambled under the bed and searched fruitlessly. I suddenly remembered that Roger used to keep a spare house key in his wallet, as did my father. Maybe it was a guy thing. Still crouched on the floor, I pulled Eddie's worn leather wallet from the back pocket, flipped it open, and wildly stuck my finger in all the compartments. I found a gold Schlage key behind his driver's license.

I glanced at Eddie. He didn't seem to be sleeping as deeply now. After all the beer, I knew it would be only a moment or two before he would wake to pee. I had to get out. But I also had to know if Zoe Hayes was inside that cage. I started to pull away the sheet.

"Hey!" Eddie murmured. "What are you doing?" He propped himself up on his elbows. My heart stopped.

"All right, Little Miss Nosey. Go ahead. Have a look," he said.

I had nothing to lose. I shut my eyes and slowly drew the sheet away.

"Isn't she a beauty?"

I slowly opened my eyes.

It was a go-cart.

"Took me three weeks to put that baby together," Eddie said, beaming. "Full suspension. Three-point-five-horsepower engine." He rolled off the bed and ran his hands over the go-cart's metal frame. "I made it for Tracey, my brother's kid. She wants to be a race car driver when she grows up. And an FBI agent. And a ballet dancer. Last time she was here she changed her getup three times." Eddie stood up. "That reminds me. I gotta do a wash. She left some of her stuff here and I told my brother I'd throw it in the wash."

I exploded in tears. Eddie put his arm around me. "Hey," he murmured. "What's all this?" He kneaded my shoulder. "Are you okay?"

"It's just that . . ." What could I say? Oh, Eddie, I'm so very relieved you're not the Long Island Kennel Killer? And I just engaged in a gratuitous sex act with you?

". . . I've never seen such a beautiful go-cart."

Eddie walked me to the door. "Hey, thanks for the treat," he said, touching my hair.

"Think nothing of it."

He chuckled. "Cute."

I turned to face him. "No, Eddie, I'm serious. I don't want you to think about any of it. Don't think about us." I knew I could never be with him again. Maybe he wasn't the serial killer after all, yet I'd suspected him, and that's reason enough to end things now.

Eddie stuck a finger in my belt loop and pulled me toward him. "Let me know if you change your mind." He put his mouth on mine and gave me what I knew would be our last kiss.

'Til next time,

V

April 28

Kevin called. My printer is ready. By the time I made it to his apartment complex, my makeup had melted and I was soaked in sweat (the A/C on the Jeep broke down last week and I couldn't afford to have it fixed). I took a rickety elevator up to the second floor, then walked down a narrow hallway saturated with a mélange of smells from many kitchens.

I found Kevin's apartment at the very end: 2B. He greeted me cheerfully and invited me in. I told him I didn't have much time. "Give a guy a break," he said playfully. "We don't get a lot of womenfolk in these parts. Please. You'd be doing me an enormous favor."

He bowed and waved his arm with a flourish. His apartment smelled like Thanksgiving and looked just as I'd pictured it—a mess of disabled technology. Computers with their guts laid bare, dismantled fax machines, broken desktop copiers, heaps of technical magazines and instruction manuals, cans of compressed air to blast away dust, tangles of cables and wires. If it had been my apartment, I'd be apologizing for the mess, but Kevin behaved comfortably. He was barefoot. His feet looked soft and delicate, like a child's.

"You've got to taste this," he said, gently setting an old aluminum pie tin on the table. "I made it myself." He peeled off the aluminum foil. "Sweet potato pie. My mom's recipe." He lifted a forkful to my lips and I suddenly felt shy. It was such an intimate and tender gesture. And it was so nice to be with a sweet, normal man for a change.

I opened my mouth and he gently slid the fork in. "It's delicious," I said. "Really incredible."

Kevin beamed. "I know." He grabbed another fork and we dug into the pie together.

Then excused himself and this time I heard it: the buzz. I'm sure it came from the bathroom. What could he possibly be doing in there? Shaving? Drilling holes? Using a vibrator (but why? and how?). A few moments later, I heard a flush and then the sound of water in the sink. I pretended to leaf through one of his electronics magazines.

"Hey, before I forget, I've got something for Pete." He pulled a shopping bag from what was originally designated as a living room. I looked inside. It was filled with broken Game Boys, radios, and Palm Pilots. On the top of the pile was a pair of plastic goggles and a small screwdriver set. "I get this stuff from suppliers, use it for components. I thought he'd enjoy fiddling around with it."

"Thanks! I'm sure he'll love it." I probably shouldn't have said anything else, but my curiosity was like that of a hyperactive two-year-old. "Hey, Kevin, I was just wondering . . ." I started. "The last couple of times you, you know, excused yourself, I heard a sort of buzzing sound coming from the bathroom. Is that some kind of electronic gadget, I don't know, some state-of-the-art computer thingamajig you've got there? I'm just dying to know."

"I've got an artificial sphincter, Valerie."

Oh God. "I'm so sorry, Kevin, it was none of my business, please forget I ever asked anything. God, I'm such an idiot!" I felt the blood rush to my neck and face.

He sat down and smiled. "No, no, don't be silly. It's a fair question, and I'm not embarrassed to talk about it. I guess it would have come up eventually if we became closer." Kevin went on to tell me that he accidentally shot off part of his lower intestine and rectum in an unfortunate accident involving his college roommate's handgun. "That's the real reason I dropped out of Michigan after my freshman year. There's a cuff around my anal canal. Most of those cuffs inflate on their own but it takes about ten minutes, and that's a little too long, so I got the kind with the electric pump. Ten minutes is a long time when you have a lovely lady waiting for you in the living room." He winked at me.

I know this sounds hardhearted, but I really don't want to date a man with a fake ass.

'Til next time,

V

April 28, continued

I went to the health club to sweat off Kevin's sweet potato pie and ran into The Incredible Shrinking Anna Fletcher, whose son Eli is in Pete's Tiger Cub troop. I met Anna eleven years ago in a stress management seminar I was leading at the public library. She weighed probably close to 200 pounds. I'd watched her slide up and down the scale for years, thin as a whippet some months, other months so fat that even her back had cleavage. Today Anna is a fit size 12 and has remained so for five or six years.

I figured she went on a liquid diet, or had her stomach stapled, which seemed like a drastic strategy but not out of the question; at this point I'd slice my fat off with a turkey carver. I would consider anything. I had to know how Anna dropped those pounds. So I asked her.

She quickly glanced around the room, then pulled me into a corner. "How desperate are you?" she asked, her voice almost a whisper. "I mean, have you hit rock bottom?"

I recognized that phrase. It originated with Alcoholics Anonymous. Anna must be in a twelve-step program. Let's see. I recently ripped a pair of Victoria's Secret underwear with my bare hands because the elastic waistband was cutting off circulation to my lower limbs. I reached into the garbage disposal to retrieve the half a Kit Kat bar Hunter had tossed in. I picked all the marshmallow stars out of a box of Lucky Charms, then told Pete it must have been a defective batch. "I guess so," I told her.

Anna nodded sympathetically. "Listen. I've been on every diet known to man. Slim•Fast. Jenny Craig. Nutrisystem. Low carb. No carb. Cabbage soup until it was coming out of my ears. And I've joined and rejoined and spent so much time at Weight Watchers I could have worked there if I hadn't been so fat. And those weigh-ins! I'd do anything to knock off a few ounces. I'd take off my wedding band, my belt. Gosh, I even pulled out a tampon once. None of those things worked for me, not in the long run. There's only one thing that kept the weight off." I looked into Anna's lovely face and waited for her to continue. "Abstinence."

"What? You stopped having sex?" I was horrified.

"No, not that kind of abstinence." Anna laughed. "I mean, I abstained from all the foods that I loved a little too much. Chocolate, cookies, cake . . . frozen cookie dough, you know what I mean."

I sure did.

"I haven't had any of that stuff in six years, not even cake on my own birthday!"

I stared at her. "You've got to be kidding."

"It's a miracle," she said, smiling. "But that's what the Overeaters Anonymous program promises, you know. Miracles. We've got a saying. 'It works if you work it.' "

I felt panicky. I knew I'd stumbled onto the Big Answer to my Big Fat Problem, but couldn't imagine permanently parting ways with my favorite foods.

'Til next time,

V

April 29

"Did you see the paper this morning?" It was my mother, and she was breathless. "Did you?"

"No, Mom, I'm still in bed."

"Zoe Hayes is alive and well and living as a circus performer in Texas! She is a trapeze artist!"

It was 7:53. "That's incredible. So she's not dead?"

"No, no, no, she's alive, Valerie. Just like your dream. You predicted this, honey, don't you see?"

"How is it like my dream, Mom?"

"Remember? The perches? Hopping from perch to perch? And remember what it said on the X ray? It said Abilene. And that's where they found her. Abilene! Texas! She checked into the hospital after she broke her arm! The broken wing, Valerie. Don't you see?"

I ran outside in my pajamas and swiped the newspaper off the driveway. The headline: ZOE HAYES ALIVE IN TEXAS. Six paragraphs down: "Detectives credit the Hayes discovery to an e-mail tip sent by a local resident. In the e-mail, the writer described what now appears to be a psychic dream which eventually lead detectives to target the region in and around Abilene. 'We looked into every lead that came across our desk, no matter how far-fetched,' Detective Avila said. 'This lead happened to be the one that panned out.' Hayes had checked into Abilene General Hospital for the treatment of a fractured wrist, where she was recognized by an emergency room orderly. The injury was sustained during a rehearsal of her trapeze act. Police have not released the identity of the person who sent the e-mail. A spokesperson for Zoe Hayes's family confirmed that the person who provided the information will be eligible for the reward money."

The next call was from a detective, a man named

Michael Avila. He said he wants to stop by the house later to ask a few questions, "just to wrap up the investigation." What if I'm implicated somehow? What if the police think I knew all about Zoe Hayes's transformation from radiography technician to trapeze artist? I felt the blood drain to my feet. I was shaking. I had to calm myself. I searched the medicine cabinet in the downstairs bathroom for Xanax, but all I could find was Tums. Then I remembered I had tucked one pill into the small zippered compartment in my fake Kate Spade bag. I swallowed it dry.

I asked Lynette if she could take Pete for the night. "What's wrong? You sound weird." I thought about Lynette's orderly, uneventful life. I wasn't ready to tell her that I was the unidentified woman who led police to Zoe Hayes. "I'm just tired, that's all. I could use a break."

"Of course you could," she responded. "Being a single mom's gotta be a bitch." The word sounded unnatural coming from her chaste mouth. "We'd be glad to take Pete. I'll stop by with Hunter to get him. Hey! Did you hear? They found Zoe Hayes. She's alive!"

"Yes. I heard."

Lynette and Hunter appeared at my door just as Detective Avila pulled up. She arched an eyebrow at me, as if to say "So *this* is why you wanted Pete out of the house." I decided I'd better set her straight. "Lynette, this is Detective Avila. He's here to ask me a few questions." Lynette looked at me quizzically. Behind the detective's head, I mouthed, "I'll tell you later."

Lynette nodded and said, brightly, "C'mon boys. Who wants to make Rice Krispie Treats?"

Michael Avila reminded me of that hunky redheaded TV chef, the one who sounds like a cabdriver and looks like an Irish god. We spent the first fifteen minutes discussing the Zoe Hayes case. Yes, I really dreamed it. No, I didn't consider myself a psychic. No, I didn't mention the dream to anyone else except for my mother. We spent another hour talking about everything besides the Zoe Hayes case. I imagined what our offspring would look like.

He used the bathroom. I didn't hear any buzzing, thank God.

"Well," he said, reaching for his pad, "I should go now. I'm sure you're anxious to eat dinner with your husband and son." He watched me with what looked like a hopeful smile.

"I'm in the process of getting a divorce. Any day now."

"Really?" I thought he looked relieved, but I may have imagined it.

"Listen, Valerie, I'd appreciate it if you'd stick around for a while in case I have any more questions. And if there's anything you want to talk about, you can reach me on my cell phone, twenty-four/seven." He handed me his card. I ran a finger over the raised letters of his name and then it came into my mind, as involuntary as a twitch: Val Avila. It had a nice ring to it. For him, I'd change my name.

I know. I'm hopeless.

At 9 P.M. there was a reporter and cameraman on my doorstep. Someone (probably my mother) had leaked my name to the media. Now I had an excuse to call Michael Avila. I asked him if it was okay to talk to the press.

"Sure. Why not?" He paused as if he were about to say something, but didn't go on. "Okay, then, you've got my number if you need to reach me."

"And you have mine. My number, I mean. You know, if *you* need to reach *me.*"

He didn't say anything else, and I felt like a total jackass.

By 10 P.M. I was still a jackass, but a famous one. I made the top story on the nightly news. Local woman's ESP leads police to Zoe Hayes, stay tuned.

I never made it to my first OA meeting. Maybe next week.

'Til next time,

𝒱

May 3

Some version of the Zoe Hayes story has been on the front page almost every day, supplanting the usual summer stories: Drought Likely To Affect Harvests. Market Street Closed For Repairs. County Fair Draws Hundreds.

Zoe Hayes won't talk to the press, and no one in her family is granting interviews. An attorney working for the Hayes family said that I was entitled to the reward money. At first I didn't want to take it—it seemed so tacky, and besides, the woman is alive—but Mom convinced me that I had no choice but to accept the reward. My bank statement came today. My mother is right. I've decided, though, that after I pay off my bills and stash a little money away, I'm going to do something charitable with the rest of it. Assuming there's anything left.

'Til next time,

V

May 5

I'm scared to be alone in the house. I'm thinking of getting a watchdog. I should probably just sell the house. The problem is, we're in the best school district in the city, and there's nothing for sale in our area right now, except for the Miller house, but they don't have a basement and I refuse to live in a house without a basement. Where would we go in case of a tornado?

I haven't been able to sleep normally in weeks. My

shrink wants to put me on Ambien, but I really don't want to take any more pills. My mother says I'll be fine just as soon as the divorce is final.

'Til next time,

V

May 8

Yet another phone call for Valerie Ryan, psychic. This time it was an assistant producer at *Good Morning America*. So far I've had calls from *People* magazine, the *Chicago Tribune*, and *The Today Show*. I know I should be excited (or at least amused) by this sudden celebrity, but I'm not. The attention is unwelcome. I have no interest in being on TV, and not only because it will make me look fifteen pounds fatter. I wish these people would leave me alone.

Roger called me and asked, "If you're so psychic, why don't you predict what I'm going to do to my girlfriend tonight?"

My old boss Cadence Bradley (aka Amazon.bitch) phoned too. I naively assumed she'd called to congratulate me. "I hear you're quite the celebrity," she began, in a tone that suggested she hadn't seen or read anything about me, but only heard this from someone in the office. Cadence is the type of person who prides herself on an ability to remain unsullied by popular culture, unreachable by its messengers.

She doesn't watch TV (except PBS), doesn't listen to radio (except NPR), and never goes to the movies (except art films). She lives in our community but refuses to subscribe to the local paper.

"How are you, Cadence?" I asked.

"I'm calling to see that you do not mention your past affiliation with the Center," she said. "We don't want our organization to be associated with any of your . . . paranormal experiences."

'Til next time,

V

May 9

I just heard from a woman who says her husband has been missing since July 1993. She has his picture posted on milk cartons, even went to a fortune-teller she'd found in a tent at the Universal Studios fake Arabian village in Orlando. "The lady said she was pretty sure Fred was the victim of spontaneous combustion," the woman told me. "But I think he ran out on me." She said she read about me in the paper and I'm her last hope. I explained that I didn't consider myself a psychic; even if I did have a touch of ESP, I couldn't marshall it on command. She thanked me extravagantly just for taking her number.

Someone else called to ask if I could help locate his lost bowling trophy.

'Til next time,

V

May 10

I had a meeting with Omar Sweet early this morning. It's official: Roger will not be charged with bigamy or statutory rape. There's not enough evidence to convict him. "The case won't hold water," Omar told me wearily. "He's the original Teflon man. Nothing sticks."

The good news, however, is that it's almost certain I'm entitled to all of Roger's undisclosed assets, and I'm likely to win full custody of Pete. "You're a hero," he told me. "You're the woman who found Zoe Hayes."

'Til next time,

V

May 11

It's over. The rotted shipwreck has finally sunk. Roger Tisdale and Valerie Ryan, according to the laws of this state and as certified by Judge Harry Mendelsohn, are officially, and rather anticlimactically, divorced.

The papers came in the mail this morning. I expected registered mail, certified mail, Federal Express, something with a little more pomp and ceremony. Instead, I found the envelope stuffed in my mailbox along with the electric bill, the church newsletter, and the ever-reproachful Victoria's Secret catalog.

Decree of Marriage Dissolution and Settlement Agreement. The end of a marriage reduced to four-teen sheets of paper and a few teaspoons of black ink. The settlement agreement detailed the division of property. I get the house and most of its furnish-ings, plus the Jeep, the big-screen TV, my iMac, and half of the $61,452 in savings and investments. Roger gets the van, the condo on Lake Merle, the weedy two acres we bought and never developed outside of Grand Haven, the broken-down speed-boat we've had in storage since 1993, the other two TVs, the Gateway and the laptop. Everything I brought to the marriage (my mother's silverware, my Todd record collection) is once again solely mine, and everything Roger brought to the marriage (the Cuisinart, the stereo, the hideous wooden mask in the family room, and the even more hideous vaginal sculpture fashioned from a tree stump) is, mercifully, once again his.

I quickly searched the document for "the guillo-tine," as Omar called it, the clause that would to de-stroy Roger if he lied under oath about his assets. I found it in the middle of the last page. "Each party has testified that s/he has been truthful about all cur-rent assets, in all forms, including but not limited to, cash, stocks, mutual funds, bonds, artwork, precious metals and other holdings valued at more than $1,000. In the event that either party has misrepresented aforementioned current assets, the court will award the sum total of those holdings to the other party."

In other words: Liar loses all.

Omar had craftily devised this delicious clause *after* Roger swore under oath that he had no holdings beyond our shared property, bank accounts, and investments. Cocksure Roger, certain that we'd never succeed in uncovering his fortunes, agreed to the clause with barely discernible hesitation.

Omar called a half hour ago. On Monday we'll meet with Libby Taylor to review her file on Roger one last time. Omar explained that he authorized Libby to continue investigating Roger after she submitted her first report. "There's every reason to believe that Roger has continued transacting business on his accounts," Omar explained. "I wanted to make sure we didn't miss anything."

I don't like the fact that Omar kept Libby on retainer without my approval. Between his fees and hers, I'll be in debt the rest of my life. Omar has assured me that his guillotine clause is foolproof, but I'm afraid I don't share his confidence.

'Til next time,

V

May 12

Detective Avila, as in "please-call-me-Michael" Avila, called today. "To discuss the Zoe Hayes case?" I asked.

"Actually, no."

I tingled with anticipation. "What did you have in mind, then?"

"I was hoping we could meet for coffee. Get to know each other."

"That sounds nice."

"How does Saturday night work for you?" he asked.

Not wanting to appear as eager as I felt, I told him I'd call him back. I said I needed to check my date book. I felt a little guilty using that old ploy, but I will always be my mother's daughter, and my mother always told me: Don't make it too easy.

'Til next time,

ꝺ

May 13

I went to my first OA meeting today. Couldn't shake the feeling that I was peeping in on some sort of secret society. It was weird but also kind of cool. Still, I'm not sure I belong. For one thing, they consider compulsive overeating a disease. Do I really think I've got a disease? Or is it a bad habit? And what about "abstinence"? Do I really want to give up sweets cold turkey? After the meeting, Anna slipped a brochure in my hand and said she hoped I come back next week. I told her I needed some time to digest everything. So to speak.

Roger materialized without warning late this afternoon. (Thankfully, Pete was around the block with Jamison, a new friend from the scouts.) He drove up in a new silver Lexus SUV with a new girlfriend in the passenger seat. He came to pick up the stereo and his CDs. I expected his girlfriend to stay in the car, but she pushed the door open even before he turned off the motor.

"You must be Roger's ex. I'm Kelia. It's Hawaiian." Her voice was silky, Southern and young. She extended a hand with annoying self-assuredness. "A pleasure." She gestured toward the flower bed by the front path. "I just adore your cosmos. And your roses! Gorgeous." She bent over and cradled one plump blossom in her hand. "I'm afraid the Japanese beetles have destroyed mine. Very sad."

She had waist-length straight blond hair with blonder highlights. She wore no discernible makeup and didn't need to. Her skin was tanned, unblemished. Her hazel eyes were rimmed with dark lashes, her lips naturally pink and full. As if nature hadn't been generous enough, the girl had dimples, two of them. She wore knee-length khaki shorts festooned with pockets, drawstrings, and Velcro tabs, and even through these baggy clothes I could see the curve of her perfect ass. She wore a handkerchief top held aloft by two thin straps, clearly no bra. Pink flip-flops, tanned feet, pink toenail polish, two toe rings, one tattoo over the left ankle bone. A dolphin. She was twenty-two, maybe twenty-three years old. She looked like she belonged on a surfboard, not in land-locked Midwestern suburbia.

Roger strode ahead toward the front door. He looked comfortable and happy. He wore baggy shorts like hers, an Abercrombie T-shirt, and Birkenstocks. "I'll be just a few minutes, sweetheart," he called out. "Why don't you ladies get to know each other?"

I had nothing to say. I wanted to run back in the house, but I didn't want to be alone with Roger. Surfer Girl continued to talk, apparently oblivious to the inherent awkwardness of the situation. I learned that she's a yoga instructor, loves vanilla soy milk, broke her toe last year snowboarding, loves doing laundry, aced her SATs, once dated Freddy Prinze Jr., is reading up on tantric sex, has an extensive collection of troll dolls, doesn't consider herself a feminist, wants to move to California. She said she met Roger in Target. (She was in the men's department buying a pair of silk boxers for herself, and he asked her to help him pick out a pair. His opening line, as he ran his hands across his crotch, was, "What size do you think I'd be?") The girl continued talking as Roger loaded the stereo and a box of CDs into the Lexus. He tossed a CD case toward me. It landed on the grass at my feet. "You can keep this one."

I glanced down at the CD. It was the Bruce Springsteen CD I'd bought Roger for Father's Day. "I never really liked him anyway," he said, slamming down the SUV's back door. "He's so . . . old." He ambled over to the girl and reached for her hand. "Come, my sweet. The movie starts in twelve minutes." He put a hand on the small of her back and moved her gently toward the curb.

"You know, Rog," drawled the girl as she tilted her head to appraise me, "you were right. She *does* look like my mom. She really does."

Roger tilted his own head and squinted. "Yes, it's a remarkable resemblance, isn't it? Except that your mother hasn't let herself go." He pulled her toward him and kissed her hungrily. He slid a hand down the back of her shorts and stared at me. "Eat your heart out," he said, and the girl laughed and playfully swatted him on the arm.

"Come on, honey," she giggled, "leave her alone."

"My pleasure," Roger said. "That has always been my goal, after all." I gulped back my rage and turned away. At that point I had only this thought to console me: The guillotine clause.

'Til next time,

𝒱

About the Author

Debra Kent writes the Diary of V for *Redbook* and Women.com and has contributed to such magazines as *Cosmopolitan, Family Circle, Mademoiselle* and *Mc-Call's*. She lives with her husband and children in the Midwest.

Now that she's single again, will V stop getting in touch with her inner Martha Stewart and connect with her inner vixen instead? Will Detective Michael Avila turn out to be Mr. Perfect? Or is it time to get to know the wildly sexy man around the corner? And with Roger up to his usual dirty tricks, will the guillotine clause save V from destitution?

V's intimate life story goes on in . . .
THE DIARY OF V: *Happily Ever After?*
Coming in October 2001
from Warner Books.

STELLAR ROMANTIC SUSPENSE
FROM
RACHEL LEE

After I Dream
(0-446-60-654-5)

Before I Sleep
(0-446-60-653-7)

When I Wake
(0-446-60-655-3)

and coming in November 2001,

Under Suspicion
(0-446-60-962-5)

"*A Rush of Wings* grabs you from the first sentence and doesn't let go. . . . Phoenix is one of the best new talents I have seen coming into literature in decades."

—*New York Times* bestselling author Dean Wesley Smith

"A goth urban fantasy that moves as fast as its otherworldly characters. A bit like *The Crow* crossed with *The Silence of the Lambs* crossed with a voice that is Phoenix's own, *A Rush of Wings* is decadent, glittering fun, wrapped up in leather and latex."

—Justine Musk, author of *BloodAngel*

"*A Rush of Wings* is a dark, rich, sensual treat . . . a perfect blend of suspense, romance, and lyrical prose to keep readers up until late, late at night turning pages. I can't wait to read more."

—Jenna Black, author of *The Devil You Know*

"If vampires didn't exist, we'd have to invent them. To do that deed, I'd recommend Adrian Phoenix."

—Gerald M. Weinberg, author of *The Aremac Project*

"An impressive first novel . . . deliciously dark . . . a real gothic treat."

—LoveVampires.com

"*A Rush of Wings* smoothly combines a serial killer police investigation with vampires and mad scientists . . . a heated romantic thriller."

—BookCrossing.com

"Adrian Phoenix has hit the jackpot with her first full-length novel. *A Rush of Wings* is a very dark, gothic, and original tale that will no doubt have readers of urban fantasy begging for more."

—ParanormalRomance.org